G000022303

Echoes In The Mist

A haunting secret from the past

Claire Voet

First published in 2021 by
Blossom Spring Publishing.
Echoes In The Mist © 2021 Claire Voet.
All rights reserved under International
Copyright Law.
Contents and/or cover may not be reproduced
in whole or in part without the express written
consent of the author.
ISBN 978-1-8383864-6-7
Names, characters, places and incidents, are either
products of the author's imagination or are used
fictitiously, save those that are in the public domain.

For René, my husband, my best friend, my soul mate and my inspiration! xx

A rose so sweet and complete is a rose as pure as a dove, speaking a language only known to love!

Claire Voet

.

Chapter One

Foaming waves hurled themselves against black volcanic sand and dark coloured rocks below. She stood precariously on the edge of a grass covered clifftop staring out to sea, wearing a black, elegant, long sleeved dress, complemented by a lengthy necklace of pearls. And her hair, dark and stylishly curled, was tucked neatly under a chic, snug fitting cloche hat, also black to match her low heeled shoes.

The sky was a thunderous swirl of pinks, reds and yellows which seemed to blend in and reflect against the surroundings of the exotic flowers and plants in the garden behind her. In the distance a dog howled sensing danger approaching. The air had become heavy and a thick mist suddenly rolled in from the sea, engulfing her, reaching every inch of the garden. She turned around with fear in her dark eyes. Echoes of voices could be heard in the mist, all talking at once. Bewildering. What were they saying? It was too fast to comprehend. She wanted to call out and make them stop but couldn't find her words. And then, they all ceased at once; giving way to a man's voice she recognised only too well.

'*Espe! Espe! Donde estas? – Espe!*' His tone was demanding, loud and of discontent.

A scream of terror penetrated piercingly through the eerie, curling, fingers that dragged her deeper into the mist...

Asleep, Jen threw out an arm with the words *Espe! Espe!* ringing in her ears. She woke with her heart pounding profusely and her nightdress soaked from perspiration. The woman's scream was still so alarmingly clear. She lay panting, gaining her breath and then it all suddenly came flooding back to her. Sitting bolt upright, the stark reality of Grace's death hit her like a truck at full speed. It took a few moments for her to calm down and come to her senses.

The dream, not that it bared any relation to Grace or her death, resembled a supernatural encounter. The man's voice had been calling *Espe* - what did *Espe* mean? She recognised his accent to be Spanish, but the woman's face she had already forgotten—other than her deep fearful eyes.

The alarm clock buzzed and flashed 7.15am. Jen gave it a bash before it would buzz again. She must have slept through its first attempt to wake her or maybe not, maybe David had turned it off. She rolled over and noticed he was gone and then she heard the shower running in their bathroom en-suite. Flopping back on her pillow she sighed wearily, the thought of dragging herself out of bed and going to work seemed an impossible task.

A feeble afternoon sun broke through a crack in a blanket of endless grey, casting a momentary golden glow over the school playing fields. The desolate trees—their leaves long gone, lining the symmetrical playing fields, swayed in the bitter cold wind. Within seconds the sun would disappear behind the gloomy clouds again and soon it would be almost dark.

She had survived the day. Jennifer Brown, known to everyone as Jen, stared aimlessly out of the window lost in thought.

"Miss! Miss!" A skinny, teenage girl, with dark hair scrapped back into a ponytail, tapped her teacher lightly on the arm.

Jen turned around, trying to drag her thoughts quickly back to the job in hand, which was teaching a class of secondary school kids English literature, something she had done for twenty-six years and had wondered on many occasions how she'd lasted that long.

The girl looked annoyed and was impatient to leave class. The other pupils were already packing up ready to go and the school bell was about to ring.

"What day do we 'ave to 'and in our essay?"

Jen raised her voice above the chatter for the others to hear her reply.

"Essays in by Thursday, which means Thursday and not Friday!"

Their groans were soon faded by the deafening bell.

After the class had dispersed, Jen sighed heavily and picked up a stack of papers on her desk to take home and mark. There had to be more to life than this. She felt as if her life was slipping away, day after day in a job she no longer had a passion for. Each day seemed long and arduous. What if she were to die, having accomplished nothing other than being a wife to a man who hardly noticed her, a mother to Alison who was away at university and didn't really need her anymore and a teacher that no longer seemed appreciated? It was like something was missing, life was incomplete. Surely at fifty years old she was not too old to have an adventure, do something different with her life? Her gloomy thoughts led her back to her best friend Grace's sudden death a few days ago. Even though her life had been cut devastatingly short, at fifty-two years old, at least she had done something with it, moved to Tenerife, had a bit of fun before she died.

Jen closed the classroom door and made her way down the corridor. Kate, the school secretary, spotted Jen from a far and called out to her. Jen didn't reply, having not heard her, so Kate quickened her step to catch up with her.

"Jen, are you OK?" She gently grabbed her arm.

Jen appeared startled, being dragged away from her thoughts yet again.

"Sorry, didn't mean to make you jump," Kate grimaced and pushed a strand of dark hair behind her ear, it immediately bounced back. Her tight curls were unruly, having just walked across a windy playground. Jen looked at her with a forlorn expression through her pale blue eyes. Her creamy coloured skin had no wrinkles at all, only a few crow's feet around the eyes and a smattering of freckles on her nose that kept her looking youthful, as did her trim figure. Her long auburn hair, with no grey strands, thanks to her regime of colouring it regularly, was loosely tied up in a bun and wispy curls framed her pretty round face. Finding it hard to find her words, for fear she would cry, Jen just nodded.

Kate gave a small sympathetic squeeze of her arm. "I know it's hard—she was—well Grace was one in a million and none of us can believe she's gone. I mean to go like that, so suddenly—a..." She whispered the words *heart attack*, as if it might be contagious if she said it too loud.

Jen, still silent, tried to pull herself together and focus. Kate continued. "Jen, why don't you take some time off work. Mr Hawkins will understand." She jerked a thumb over her shoulder towards the headmaster's office.

Jen finally found her voice. "He's already offered for me to take time off and I will soon. I'm fine. I've had the weekend to shed plenty of tears."

Kate pushed her bright blue rimmed glasses back up her nose. "One weekend is not enough. I know how close you were to Grace when she worked here and I remember her moving to Tenerife was tough on you."

A ghost of a smile crept across Jen's lips. "Not that tough, I had some really good holidays visiting her." An image of herself arriving at Grace's villa flashed into her mind. Last summer when Jen and David had argued after her finding out he had used a large chunk of their savings towards buying a new car without even discussing it and had cancelled their holiday without so much as an apology, Jen had packed a suitcase and went to stay with Grace in Tenerife. Bubbly, cheerful, Grace. She had never married, never found Mr Right, perhaps a blessing Jen had said to her on many occasions, as there probably was no such thing as a Mr Right, if her own husband was anything to go by.

She should have been visiting her this summer. The thought of never seeing Grace again was heart breaking. She quickly swallowed the lump forming at the back of her throat and concentrated on Kate.

Kate frowned. "What will happen to her villa out there? Does she have any family—

brothers or sisters?

"No. None at all and that is where it gets complicated."

Kate raised her eyebrows. "Complicated, how?"

A few stragglers pushed by as they hurried down the corridor, gym kits spilling out of their school bags, chatting animatedly and laughing.

"Not here. Can we go somewhere quieter?" Jen suddenly had an idea. "David is out on a pool tournament tonight, are you free?"

Kate hesitated for a moment, trying to remember what she had planned to cook for dinner. Was it something she could throw in the oven and be out early enough?

"Sorry—it's short notice—don't worry."

Kate shook her head. "No...of course I can come round. I'll bring a bottle of wine. And I'll get a taxi?" she added.

Jen smiled with relief, she needed a friend to speak to right now. "On a school night?" she said wryly, with reference to the bottle of wine. "Yes, on a school night! These are desperate times, which calls for desperate measures! Seven thirty OK?"

Jen checked her watch, she had enough time to get the pile of marking done that was wedged under her arm and grab a microwave curry. "Perfect!" She replied and then dashed off.

The crunch of tyres on the gravel outside, spurred Jen to rush to the window. Pushing back the net curtain, she could see the snow coming down sideways in the yellow headlights of the taxi. She ran to open the front door and let Kate in from the cold.

Laden with two bottles of wine, one red and one white, Kate hurried into the house with snowflakes melting into her mass of hair.

"Thank you!" Jen took the wine and her long blue coat that matched her glasses, and the two women went into the living room.

"This is cosy!" It was the first time Kate had seen the room since it had been decorated. She glanced around approvingly, her eyes stopping on the open fire that crackled invitingly, giving a warm orange glow that seemed to bounce off the neutral tones of the two beige sofas, matching cushions and equally matching, fluffy rugs; draped fashionably in all the right places. On the wall was a family portrait of Jen, David and their daughter Alison, when she was five years old.

"Red or white?" Jen held up both for Kate to choose.

"Your choice. I couldn't remember what you like so I brought both. Kate grinned and then made a beeline for the large rubber plant in the corner standing so tall that it almost reached the ceiling. "Wow!" What a beauty! I'm useless with plants. This wasn't here before you decorated was it?"

Jen shook her head. "It was in the conservatory, but, as David has decided to turn that into a pool room now, I had to move it in here because there was no room for it. Poor thing."

Jen returned to the kitchen and called out. "I love plants. If I had my way the house would be full of them."

A moment later she walked back in the room and handed Kate a glass of red. "Tropical plants like in the Canaries," she added.

"Which brings us to the subject of..." Kate said with a grimaced look.

Jen sighed, "Yep." She knew full well she was referring to Grace.

Kate sat down on the sofa and Jen followed suit, next to her. "She took a sip of wine for courage. Talking about Grace was so painful. "A translator from the police called me on Friday afternoon to tell me about Grace's death," she began.

"Oh so that's how you found out?"

Jen nodded. "Apparently, Grace's neighbour, a dear lady, who I've met a couple of times now—Mrs Schneider—she's German by the way in case you haven't guessed— anyway um—oh God this is so hard—she found —she found her." Jen brushed away a tear with the cuff of her jumper.

Kate reached out and touched her hand. "What did the translator say?" she asked gently, encouraging her to continue.

"Just that my telephone number was in the back of Grace's passport as the person to contact in an emergency. They think she may have had a heart attack, they found a bottle

9

of blood pressure pills that were newly prescribed in the bathroom cabinet." Jen was crying openly now, unable to control her emotions any longer.

"Oh poor Grace." Kate reached out and hugged Jen. Her crying then turned into a heartfelt sob. "Let it all out. It's OK." Kate rubbed her back in comfort.

Eventually, Jen pulled away and looked up with a mascara stained face. "They asked me to go there and arrange what happens with her bod…" she couldn't bring herself to finish her sentence.

Kate looked taken aback. "Gosh! Really?

"Well she doesn't have anyone else and I'm, was—her only closest friend."

"What will you do? I mean will you bring her back here? Did Grace ever speak about if the worst should happen?"

"Not really. I know she said once that she didn't want a funeral, people all being miserable and glum and would rather they give money to a charity than waste it on flowers. But she was quite tipsy at the time. She said it jokingly about falling in the pool and should she have drowned after too many glasses of wine." Jen smiled, remembering that evening. It had been so much fun, they had enjoyed a BBQ and polished off quite a substantial amount of wine. Sometimes the best nights were the ones when they just stayed in and chatted about anything and everything. They were great memories she would treasure forever.

"Grace was a person who didn't like a fuss. I could imagine she meant it," Kate said, thoughtfully.

"Yes she probably did." Jen dabbed her eyes with a screwed up tissue she had been nursing in the palm of her hand.

"Look at us two, what a mess." Kate wiped her own tears. "Do you want me to come with you?"

"To Tenerife?" Jen blew her nose and then took a sip of wine. "Yes. I can try and get time off work, I know it's a bit last minute but I could ask."

"No it's fine Kate. Thanks, but I'll be alright. I've got Mrs Schneider over there. She'll have one of her freshly baked cakes or homemade bread waiting for my arrival, I daresay. Bless her." She smiled through her tears. "In a way it will be comforting to go back—I will feel close to Grace; a chance to say goodbye properly. It's something I need to do alone."

"I understand. We could have a little memorial for her at school when you get back," Kate said, the idea just entering her head.

"That's a lovely idea."

Kate took a swig of wine. "So when are you going?"

"At the weekend. I've booked a week off work." She suddenly looked worried. "I hope it's enough time, there'll be a lot to do over there."

"Well if it's not, you will just have to stay

longer," Kate replied with a shrug of her shoulders.

"Yes, David would love that." She rolled her eyes.

"What does David say about it all? I guess he can't get time off to go with you?"

Jen gave a sarcastic hoot. "Even if he could, he wouldn't come with me. He never liked Grace, but then again he doesn't like anyone unless they are from the bank. He also doesn't like travelling, so he wouldn't sit on a plane for over four hours."

David only ever wanted to go to Devon or Cornwall, which was where they went when Alison was a child, year after year. Now that she was grown up and at university, in her final year of studying a Bachelor's degree in art and design. Jen had persuaded David for them to broaden their horizons with their holidays. However, the last one to the Costa Del Sol was uneventful and boring, so much so that she had read five books during their holiday! She would rather have gone to Tenerife and visit Grace. They always had fun. She was going to miss her and visiting that beautiful island. It was a world away from England. A world away from her boring life. Those trips were her chance to escape and now they had come to an abrupt end, just like poor Grace's life.

The mist was thick and heavy, rolling in again from the sea. The young woman, dressed in black, appeared through it as if by magic. Bewildered. Distressed. And with a sudden harrowing cry she fell to her knees sobbing, clutching at a single pink rose, tearing each petal, tossing them around her like she was performing a ritual, each one falling to the ground before being swallowed up by the mist. Eventually, she too disappeared, although her cries continued to echo through the murky dismal blanket of grey.

Jen turned her head, restless in the arm chair and then woke, gasping for breath. It took her a moment to realise she had been dreaming and she must have dosed off after Kate had left, having polished off most of the wine. She heaved herself out of the chair, turned off the lights and made her way upstairs to bed, she would clear up the glasses and empty bottles in the morning. David was not home yet, she sighed walking into their bedroom, too tired to even care.

It was Thursday evening when Jen finally saw David. He had hardly been home, dashing in and out with just a *hello, is my white polo shirt clean?* And *no time for dinner, I'll grab something when I'm out.* He would, however, always plant a dutiful kiss on her cheek before rushing out of the house. If he wasn't going to a pool night organised by the bank, it was 'the bank's' quiz night or 'the bank's' bowling night, or some other event organised by 'the bank.' Whatever it was, Jen was never invited and even if she had been, she wouldn't have gone. It was bad enough suffering 'the bank's' Christmas dinner party, which was always dreadfully boring, but fortunately it was only once a year.

The aroma of lasagne and garlic bread filled the whole house when David arrived home.

"Jen! Jen!" He dropped his briefcase in the hallway and rushed to find her. She was in the kitchen pouring herself a glass of wine.

"Jen, you are not going to believe this!"

She looked at him, surprised by his sudden burst into the kitchen. "What am I not going to believe?" She placed the wine glass down and stood with her hands on hips waiting for his reply, wondering what it was this time—'the bank' won the bowling tournament—'the bank' was going to organise a trip to the moon! Whatever it was, it would be something to do with 'the bank' that, she was certain of. And she was right. But it wasn't quite the trivial news she had expected.

"I've been offered a promotion, Managing Director." He ran over to her and without warning, kissed her on the lips, before picking her up and swinging her around like a lightweight rag doll, for which Jen was not amused and didn't enjoy a second of his new found affection towards her—if you could call it that.

She shrieked with annoyance. "David, put me down!"

He placed her back down on her feet. After gaining her breath, and having seen how happy he was, she felt mean not to share just a modicum of his excitement. "Wow! I mean that's great." She hoped she sounded genuine enough. "What about Graham Harris? Where's he going then—if you are taking his job?" She turned her back on him to check the dinner in the oven and to try and hide her lack of enthusiasm.

"Nowhere, silly. I've been offered a transfer. That's the most exciting part of my news."

She slammed the oven door and turned to face him again. "Where?" she asked, folding her arms. As long as it was within commuting distance that would be fine, but she had no intention of moving to a new house, especially as they had just decorated.

"Bournemouth," he announced, helping himself to a beer from the fridge.

She sighed with relief. "Right, well still commutable then from Andover. Dinner will be ready in about two minutes." She opened the cutlery drawer and took out the knives and forks.

He looked at her in disbelief. "It's a bloody hour's drive from here and probably more than that during rush hour." He took a swig of his beer and sat down at the kitchen table. "There's some lovely areas we could live in— doesn't have to be in Bournemouth itself. Sue—you know—mortgage advisor Sue, she says Ferndown is really nice, her aunt lives there. We'll get a bigger house, it will be

15

great!"

Jen threw the cutlery down on the table. "I don't want a bigger house. There's only the two of us now Alison has gone. I like it here, we've lived here for fifteen years."

"Exactly—long enough—time for a change." She took the dinner out of the oven and plated it up, trying hard to hold back her tears. This was all getting too much. First Grace, now David wanting to move. "And what about my job?" She placed a plate of garlic bread in the centre of the table.

He reached out and grabbed a piece, blowing his fingers at the sting of the heat. "They've got schools there—good ones. You said yourself you were getting fed up and would like a change." He devoured the piece of garlic bread.

"I meant a complete change of career, not... oh what's the point?" She plonked a plate of lasagne in front of him.

He gave it a prod with his fork, inspecting it closely and when he had swallowed his mouthful of bread he asked, "Is it shop bought?"

"Yes it's bloody shop bought. Do you really think I have the time to make a homemade one?"

"Alright, I was only asking." He picked up his knife and cut it in the centre, letting the steam out.

"In case you hadn't noticed, which of course you haven't because you are always far too wrapped up in yourself—I am grieving.

I am trying to cope with work and I have to fly to Tenerife on Saturday to sort out..." She couldn't bring herself to finish the rest of her sentence and was no longer able to hold back her tears. "I... I can't be dealing with moving on top of all this."

He sat back in his chair and ran his fingers nervously through a thatch of hair, the colour of salt and pepper. He was never very good at dealing with what he considered to be 'awkward or emotional' situations. He forced himself to reach out and pat her gently on the hand. She pulled it away abruptly, annoyed at his patronising comforting technique which was of no comfort at all. Any normal person would have given her big hug, but then David was far from normal, she was well aware of that.

"Look you don't need to think about the move right now. I don't have to start my new job until April, that's three months away. I understand, you'll want time to get used to the idea. I just wanted to share my news. Wrong timing, I know."

She didn't reply, so he dug into his dinner, realising that he was famished and hadn't eaten anything since lunchtime. She glared at him with contempt, tears still streaming down her face. How dare he drop a bombshell on her like that, knowing full well about Grace. She got up and took her plate to the bin then scrapped the contents into the rubbish.

He watched her, bemused. "It's not that

bad, although I have to say shop bought lasagne is not my favourite either."

"I threw it away because I feel sick. Sick of everything including you!"

She walked over to the table, picked up his beer and then proceeded to pour it over his head.

"What!...What the...! Have you lost your mind, woman?" He stood up from the table with beer pouring down his face.

"Yes, the day I married you! You can sleep on the sofa until I leave on Saturday." She stormed out of the kitchen leaving him dripping in beer and lost for words.

Chapter Two

The thunderous roar from the aircraft landing on the tarmac was almost deafening but short lived, followed by an applaud from its happy passengers, excited to be in Tenerife; all of them that was, apart from Jen, who felt nothing but sadness knowing that Grace wouldn't be waiting for her like she always was.

A deep, husky voice broke into Jen's sombre thoughts. *"Ladies and Gentlemen, this is your captain speaking, welcome to Tenerife. On behalf of myself, my co-pilot and the cabin crew, we would like to wish you a safe onward journey and a lovely holiday. For those of you who are lucky enough to call Tenerife home, welcome home!"*

Why do all pilots sound so damn sexy? She managed a small smile, Grace would have agreed with her on that one. She peered out of the window again, looking at the blue sea and the barren dry landscape outside. In a strange sort of way, it did feel like home. It was all so familiar, the north of the island even more so, having spent numerous holidays there with Grace.

It wasn't long before Jen had gone through passport control, claimed her suitcase and was on her way. It was busy as always, travel representatives holding up boards with names, private taxi drivers lined up amongst friends and family waiting to greet their loved ones. A sudden outburst of raucous laughter and screaming came from behind. She turned around to see a party of ten women in their early to mid twenties, dressed in mini skirts, stilettos and pink *kiss me quick* hats edged with fur, running towards a group of other women who had arrived on an earlier flight, all wearing the same hats. At the front of the line was a pretty brunette wearing a pink sash that read *"Bride To Be."*

Jen watched them hug and kiss. A hen party, poor girl. Would she still be so happy after twenty-three years of marriage? They were probably on their way to Playa De Las Americas for a week of sunbathing and partying, lucky sods. What she would give to be one of those girls right now. Not only to be thirty years younger but to have fun, to go wild and do silly things with a group of girlfriends. She wanted to reach out to her and tell her to enjoy every minute of it because it would be gone in a flash. Before the girl would know it she would soon be changing nappies, doing school runs, then waving goodbye to them as they leave home. And then suddenly left feeling over the hill, stuck with a husband who didn't really notice her anymore. Or maybe not. Maybe she would be one of the lucky ones who would have a good marriage. She hoped for her sake she was. Many marriages didn't last these days and, even if they did, what would they have left at the end of it all when they were grey and old? She suddenly realised just how cynical she had become over the years being married to David. She sighed wistfully, grabbed hold of her large bright red suitcase and continued to walk on past the crowds.

The sunshine beating down between the palm trees was the only warm greeting Jen received as she walked out of the building and made her way towards the bus stop. No Grace waiting for her this time, with her usual excitable, beaming smile, waving and calling her name. The familiar smell of subtropical plants and bougainvillea suddenly hit her and she stopped for a moment to inhale and take in the atmosphere. Under different circumstances she would have been as excited as all the other tourists were, dashing past her on their way to catch the bus or pick up their car hire.

The bus was full. Jen was lucky to have found a seat at the rear next to the window. The 343 went straight to Puerto De La Cruz, which meant that she didn't have to change at Santa Cruz. Thankfully, the air conditioning was working well and she was relieved to get out of the heat and sit down in the cool, being overly dressed having travelled from cold England. She was also grateful that her companion sitting next to her was a teenage girl; headphones stuck in her ears and her eyes glued to her phone. At least she wouldn't have to make conversation, which she had also managed to avoid on the flight over. The old man next to her had slept all the way. She flopped back in her seat and prepared herself mentally for the journey ahead, which would be just under two hours including all the stops. It would have been much easier to fly to the north airport, had they accepted more international flights instead of mainly domestic ones.

Relieved that she hadn't had one of those awful dreams she'd been having recently but, annoyed at herself for missing out on the scenic route having slept most of the way, she yawned as the bus pulled into the station at Puerto De La Cruz – Estaction De Guaguas, a big, bright, green, Canary style building.

After dragging her case from the hold below the bus, she made her way to the taxi rank. From there she took a taxi to La Paz, which was up a hill, like almost everywhere in the north of the island, owing to the landscape of past erupted volcanos and in particular,

Mount Teide. La Paz, (The Peace), just like Puerto de La Cruz, was rich with history, not that one would notice at first glance with so many new hotels and holiday apartments that had sprung up over recent years. But look closer and one would soon discover it's history in old houses tucked down little winding streets, also the stunning Botanical Gardens, the quaint little church of San Amaro and even the occasional cute looking tavern that had been open for centuries as stated above their thresholds.

Having paid the taxi driver, Jen collected her luggage and made her way along a narrow path lined with cypress trees and more sweet smelling bougainvillea. And there at the end of the path she spotted the villa, boasting two centuries of history with its thick stone walls and faded green shutters on each of the windows. The uneven steps leading to an equally faded green wooden front door, were complemented by two cheerful looking hanging baskets either side of bright pink and white petunias. Beneath a rusting bell, a chipped, floral name plate read *Villa Esperanza*. Although in need of some obvious tender loving care, the familiarity of this rambling house seemed to greet her like a dear old friend.

Chapter Three

Mrs Schneider opened the heavy wooden door. It gave a loud protesting creak. "Jen, I got your text that your flight was on time, very gut!" She smiled warmly, flashing a row of perfectly formed false teeth. Her dark hazel eyes surveyed Jen from head to toe. "Come! You must be tired after your journey." She ushered Jen in before she had the chance to reply, grabbing her suitcase and wheeling it off down the hallway into the main living area. Jen followed behind, feeling guilty that Mrs Schneider should be rolling her case, but it had all happened so fast, and she seemed insistent on helping.

"Yes, all was on time, thank goodness," Jen said at last, gazing around the familiar room. Everything looked as it always did, as if Grace had just nipped out and would be back soon. A dark red four-seater sofa, sumptuous and inviting with lots of brightly coloured scattered cushions, dominated the room. In the corner, a matching armchair, equally as inviting, was strategically placed in view of the large plasma television mounted on the wall. Over the arm of the chair was Grace's cardigan, draped exactly where she had left it, as were her flip flops placed neatly behind the chair. Magazines and a local newspaper lay on a dark oval coffee table. It had all the characteristics of an old but charming lived-in room. An aroma of something roasting in the oven wafted in from the kitchen like a welcoming embrace.

As if reading Jen's mind, Mrs Schneider said, "I thought you would be hungry after your long journey. I made you some dinner." She eyed Jen closely, observing the poor dear, she looked positively shattered, probably not slept for days, given the sudden loss of her close friend Grace.

"Oh, that's most kind, Mrs Schneider, thank you. I hope you didn't go to too much trouble. It smells wonderful!"

Mrs Schneider smiled. "Not at all." Her cheeks were rosy from cooking and her eyes seemed to twinkle like she was always smiling, even when she wasn't—which gave her an approachable vibe, like a friendly old aunt one could confide in over a cup of tea.

"It is the least I can do to help under this very sad circumstances," she added.

Jen immediately picked up on her small grammatical error but of course did not wish to correct her. In general, Mrs Schneider had remarkable English. Her German accent was hardly apparent and at times she sounded almost British.

"I tried to think what you would like to eat," she continued. "Not knowing if you would enjoy German cuisine and, I must confess that I can't cook many Canarian dishes as well as the locals do, so I thought I would play safe and opt for a British one. I remembered a dish from my days in London—Cottage Pie. It's OK with you?" She waited eagerly for Jen's reaction. And with relief she sighed as Jen grinned and replied

"Wonderful, my favourite!"

"Gut!" she said happily, giving a small appreciative clap of her hands. "Shall we go into the kitchen or do you wish to freshen up first? It is almost ready, but there's still time."

"Let's go into the kitchen. I'll have a shower later. I'll wash my hands at the kitchen sink," Jen smiled.

The kitchen was spacious and kept in a traditional style. Brass pots and pans hung above an old-fashioned cooking range. On the other side of the room stood an oak wooden table with chairs to seat six, next to glass patio doors that Grace had put in only a year ago; to give the room more light and easier access to the garden. Banana plants close to the open doors swayed in the gentle, warm breeze, brushing against the pane. Jen stepped outside and stood for a moment admiring the garden and the views. There were so many exotic plants and flowers, but she had no idea of all their names. However, she did recognise the large bush of strelitzias, also known as bird of paradise, one of her most favourite flowers and it had been Grace's too. From this elevated position it was possible to see the sun setting above the sea. She turned her head to the left in the direction of the BBQ area and the two sunbeds neatly lined up on the lawn, noticing a snow-capped Mount Teide forming a beautiful back drop to the whole scene. Amazing to think it was cold enough to snow up there—yet so warm below. The dormant volcano seemed to loom over the whole of the north of the island. She could see why Grace had bought this house; it really was special. Although this wasn't all of it, on the other side stood a sizable outbuilding. Grace had shown her it only the once. She didn't like going in there. It was cold, dusty, and needed a lot of work doing to it, if it were to become anything usable. It was certainly spacious and had potential. Grace had toyed with the idea of making it into a self-contained apartment for holiday rentals, but she wasn't sure if she wanted the inconvenience of strangers sharing the garden, and so she had abandoned the idea and hadn't managed to come up with another.

"Would you like a drink?" Mrs Schneider appeared next to Jen. "Wine maybe?" She held up a bottle of red Rioja.

"Wonderful! Thank you." Jen stepped back inside and noticed that the table was now set but only for one. She frowned. "Are you not joining me?" She turned to face Mrs Schneider.

"Oh, I couldn't possibly intrude." Mrs Schneider trotted over to the cupboard and took out a large, tall wine glass.

"Oh no, you wouldn't be intruding. If I'm honest, I would very much enjoy your company."

"In that case, I'd better set another place." She smiled, looking pleased. It was obvious that Jen needed her support, and she was happy to give it. It felt good to be useful. It had been a long time since anyone had needed her. It had also been a long time since she had dinner with anyone. She wasn't one for going out much and socialising with others. Not because she was unsociable, far from it, but more that she enjoyed her own company and didn't feel the need. She took out another wine glass for herself, filled both and handed one to Jen. Jen took a sip and then went to wash her hands at the sink.

"So, you spent some time in London?" Jen said, remembering her comment earlier. This well-spoken German lady intrigued her. She suddenly realised she knew little about her, having only met her in passing a few times when staying with Grace on holiday. She didn't even know if she was in fact married, she didn't wear a wedding ring and she had never heard her speak of a Mr Schneider, yet Grace always called her Mrs Schneider. But something Jen did know about her, was that

Mrs Schneider could bake very well. She often popped in with cakes and freshly made bread for Grace, but never stayed long and never outstayed her welcome or intruded on Grace's privacy, just as she had behaved this evening, thoughtful and respectful towards others. If her cooking was as good as her baking, which Jen suspected it was, then she was in for a treat.

"When I was young, I worked in London as an au pair," Mrs Schneider replied, setting her own place at the table. Her face lit up. "A lovely family—the Haydocks, they had three children. I worked for them until the youngest turned fifteen. I was with them for twenty years."

"That explains your good English," said Jen, taking a sip of wine.

"Oh, it's still not perfect even after all these years," Mrs Schneider blushed. She was never good at accepting compliments. "I returned to Germany after that, met a wonderful man, we married and a year later, sadly, he died—pneumonia."

"Gosh how awful for you."

"Yes, it hit me hard, we had so many plans for the future. Anyway, I decided to go back to work as I needed the money, and I found a job as a housekeeper for a very wealthy man —a surgeon in fact. His wife had left him. He was hardly at home, probably why she left him." She gave a short snoot of a laugh and then continued her story, "but when he was home, I had to cook for him. He was very

29

particular and didn't like anything other than German food. I had no chance to speak English there, he didn't like the English, he was still sour about his father being killed in the war."

"I see." Jen raised her eyebrows. "I suppose we forget there are two sides to every war."

"Indeed. His father was shot out of the sky over the British channel on a mission to attack Portsmouth. So, what do you expect would happen?" She shook her head with despair. "It was a tragedy all round and too many lives lost."

"Did you live in the house?" asked Jen, delicately swerving more conversation about the war.

"For a while but then I took a job as a clerk in an office—that wasn't really me, and so I went travelling and ended up here, that was ten years ago now." She took a sip of wine thoughtfully and then suddenly remembered the dinner. She hurried over to the other side of the kitchen and with gloved hands, pulled out a large dish of cottage pie from the oven.

Jen's stomach gave an impatient rumble, she hadn't eaten anything all day and it smelt divine! "Wow! Ten years, you must really like it here. Grace loved it here too."

"Yes, she did. This island has captured the hearts of many a tourist." She placed the glass dish down on a mat in the centre of the table, then collected two dishes of vegetables and brought them to the table. "And for many years too, Tenerife has a lot of history," she added.

"I can see why so many love it here." Jen held her plate up as Mrs Schneider spooned out succulent beef and creamy mashed potato. Her tummy rumbled again.

"Help yourself to veg." Mrs Schneider pointed to the two dishes, one of cauliflower cheese and the other of honey glazed carrots. She then topped up their wine. "They even have an English church here, All Saints, opened in 1890—and the English library opened in 1903, would you believe? Just shows how long the British have been coming here."

"Really? I never knew there was an English church or library."

"Did Grace not tell you?" Mrs Schneider served herself now.

"No. Grace was not a churchgoer and although she liked reading sometimes, she was not an avid reader, not enough to make her want to join a library. Art was her passion, as you know. She was a good art teacher. That's how we met. She worked at the school that I teach at. I teach English literature."

"Yes, I know, she told me after your last stay. I said to her she should teach here on the island, maybe turn that outbuilding into an art studio. She said she would think about it, but something seemed to be holding her back, I don't know what."

Jen frowned.

"Dig in, it will get cold," Mrs Schneider

31

said.

It was 9.30pm before they finished dinner and Mrs Schneider handed her the keys to the villa. She explained how the old boiler worked, she had the same one too, and then handed her an envelope with a note inside containing details of the morgue where Grace's body was and the name of her solicitor. Mrs Schneider noticed the pained look on Jen's face. "Don't worry, I'll come with you. They won't speak English—very little anyway, I speak enough Spanish to help you."

"Thank you, Mrs Schneider." Jen was glad of the help, knowing full well it would be a difficult morning and a difficult few days ahead.

"Try and get some rest, my dear. I'll see you in the morning at 10am, is that gut?"

"Gut, I'm mean good," Jen suppressed a chuckle and cleared her throat with a small cough, feeling slightly embarrassed at taking over her accent, although Mrs Schneider seemed oblivious. "Perfect thank you," Jen confirmed.

"By the way, I left you some homemade bread in the pantry. There's plenty of jam and cereal I noticed. And there's fresh milk in the fridge, plus two bottles of water, it's best not to drink tap water."

"Oh, that's most kind." Jen's lips stretched into a thankful smile. "What would I do without you?"

"Let's hope you won't need to find out," hooted Mrs Schneider. A moment later she was gone, and Jen found herself standing in the living room, listening to the faint chirping sound of crickets coming from outside of the window. Other than the crickets and the ticking of the clock on the wall, it suddenly felt very silent. It was strange being in Grace's home without her. She glanced over at her cardigan and her flip flops again and shuddered. Keep the mind occupied, that's the best way forward. She then looked over at her suitcase and bag leaning against the back of the sofa. Time to unpack. Grabbing hold of her bag, she flung it over her shoulder and rolled her suitcase out of the room in the direction of the guest room, where she always stayed.

The house was all on one level. The hallway was long and narrow. To the right was Grace's bedroom. The door was not quite closed, and she turned her head, not wanting to face Grace's room yet. To the left was the guest room and at the end of the hallway was the bathroom.

The guest room was bright and sunny, with yellow patterned daisy curtains and matching bedding on both twin beds. The view from the window was to the side of the house and looked out on a small path lined with more banana plants, which led down to the outbuilding.

She decided on the bed closest to the door, this was the one she normally slept in, in case she should need to go to the loo during the night. She pulled opened the doors to a large built-in wardrobe and began hanging up some of the clothes she feared would crease too much, should she leave them any longer. After that she opened the drawers below in the same wardrobe and put away her undies, the rest could wait until tomorrow. Picking out her cotton pink nightdress, white robe, and fluffy pink open toe slippers from her suitcase, which she pushed her feet into before grabbing her toiletry bag, heading off in the direction of the bathroom.

The bathroom was modern in comparison to the rest of the house. Grace had updated it only eighteen months ago. The terracotta tiles still gleamed like new as did the walk-in shower unit. It had hardly been used, given the fact that it was only for guests and Grace rarely had guests. In fact, Jen was probably the last one to have used it. Grace had her own bathroom en-suite with a large size jacuzzi bath. Having hung her night wear up on the hook at the back of the door, she picked up the soft, beige coloured bath towel from the rail and smelt it. It smelt of washing powder. She wondered if Grace had left it there for an unexpected guest at some point or had Mrs Schneider left it out for her—she suspected it had been Mrs Schneider, she was so thoughtful.

She slipped out of her clothes and pulled back the shower door—giving a sudden short gasp at the unexpected sight of a rather large, green, speckled gecko in the shower. Gazing upwards, she could see the tiny bathroom window ajar, that was obviously where it had come from. Now the question was, how to get it out? Slipping on her robe, for protection in case in the unlikely event that it lunged towards her, she picked up her toiletry bag and gave it a little nudge. It moved only a fraction, and so she tried again. This time the nudge had the desired effect. It bolted up the wall and headed back out of the window. Jen gave a sigh of relief, laughing at herself. Grace would have found that highly amusing. She was used to the wildlife on the island and seemed to have no fear, cockroaches, spiders, she never made a fuss. She placed the bottles she had found in the bathroom cabinet into the shower cubicle, turned on the shower and waited a moment until it was warm before getting in.

The water gushed out in a steady flow and it felt good between her shoulder blades and the back of her head. She stood with her hands dangling by the side of her body while the water pounded into her tired bones. When she had loosed up enough, she reached for the shampoo and lathered it into her scalp, after rinsing she applied conditioner, then finally rubbed her body with a loofah that hung on the shower head with watermelon scented shower gel.

After getting out of the shower she dried herself off, and with the corner of the towel rubbed the mirror clear from the steam. She made quick work of applying her cleanser, followed by her antiwrinkle night cream, cleaned her teeth, then slipped on her nightwear and padded down the corridor back to the bedroom to dry her hair. And finally, at 10.30pm she had made sure the house was locked, lights were off and then got into bed.

The curtain flapped gently in the breeze coming through her window. She contemplated getting up and closing it, but it was perfectly safe with security bars at the window. It was safe from humans but not from geckos or any other creatures. It would be too warm with the window closed, so it was best to leave it open, even if meant unwelcoming visitors, she decided. She needed to acclimatize to even the night temperature, it felt so warm after leaving freezing cold England that morning. Before she could think any further on the matter, her mobile phone buzzed. Alison's name flashed up on the screen. She eagerly clicked on the text.

Hi Mum, did you arrive OK? Must be weird without Grace. I hope you are going to be OK over there alone. Dad text me to see if I had heard from you. I think he's been trying to contact you to see if you got there OK.
Love you. xxx

Jen checked her mobile for more text

messages. Nothing. No missed calls either. Why ask, Alison? Why hadn't he bothered to contact her himself? Typical of David to get other people to do his dirty work. He didn't want to speak with her, that was obvious, but he did want to know she was safe, at least that was some consolation. She replied to Alison's text.

Hi Sweetheart, I got here safely thank you. Yes, it's weird without Grace. Very sad, but I'll be fine, don't worry about me. Mrs Schneider, the lady who lives next door, is helping me with everything and she is really lovely. I'll call you later in the week once I'm on top of everything.
Love you lots. xxx

There was no need to mention David or message him, if he couldn't be bothered to contact her himself, she couldn't be bothered to let him know she had arrived safely— besides, he would find out from Alison soon enough. She placed her mobile phone on the bedside table and switched off the lamp, her thoughts, annoyingly, still on David. She was surprised he had even noticed that she was gone—must be back from one of his boring bank events. She yawned and snuggled down under the sheets, her eyes felt heavy and before long she drifted off to sleep.

The room darkened, all bar the moonlight casting a slight silver shine on the figure that had appeared in the far corner. As Jen's breathing became shallower, it drifted nearer. Her eyelids flickered, aware of the feeling of being watched but far too exhausted to do anything about it. She could sense someone standing close, even a faint smell of sweet perfume, but still, she couldn't find the strength to wake up. It was if her whole body was made of led—too heavy to lift any part of it, least of all her eyelids.

Chapter Four

Puerto De La Cruz
1927

The familiar sound of an organ playing and voices singing *All Things Bright And Beautiful,* could be heard around the grounds of the All Saints Church. The morning sunlight reflected through the stained-glass windows and onto the worshipers inside the grey stone building. When the hymn had finally finished, outside birdsong took over. A blackbird and a blue chaffinch in nearby palm trees continued as if in competition with each other. Tenerife was called the island of eternal spring by the locals for good reason. The air was warm, and the sweet scent of flowers gave the impression of spring all year round. It was easy to see why there were enough Anglican worshipers to fill an entire church. They had all settled in Puerto De La Cruz, making it their new home, just like birds flocking to warmer climes. A few moments later the wooden doors opened, and the congregation filtered out—the women looking elegant in their fine dresses and stylish hats and the men smartly dressed in their Sunday best tailored suits. Children were also looking spruced up with shiny faces and neatly combed hair.

Vicar Albert Jones stood outside shaking hands and wishing them all well as one by one they dispersed into different directions, most on foot and those wealthier by motor car. He then went back inside, collected the hymn books, and placed them neatly on the table at the back of the church before disappearing off.

The loud squeak of the heavy wooden doors echoed when Mary Osborne walked in.

"Vicar!" she called out, realising he was probably outback in the vestry. She called again, a little louder this time. He suddenly appeared, while flattening his grey hair down with the palms of his hands before straightening his spectacles that were a little askew, having just removed his cassock.

Mary stood tall with her shoulders pushed back, wearing a pale pink dress that stopped fashionably just below her knees, and a navy-blue handbag, hanging from her shoulder matched her shoes perfectly. She was always impeccably dressed and not only on a Sunday. "Vicar, I wondered if I may have a word with you about Dorothy Rodriguez."

"Dorothy?" Albert frowned. *Was she sick? She seemed well when he said goodbye to her just now.*

"It's not easy for her, a widow bringing up three girls and her late husband's money is running out. She will soon have nothing to live from." Mary sighed. "She's a proud woman, she confided in me only because I coaxed it out of her. I tried to give her money, but she wouldn't accept. I wondered if there was any way the church could help."

Albert scratched his head in thought, displaying a baffled expression. "The church doesn't have spare money, Mary, and don't forget Dorothy is a proud woman, I can't imagine she would be seeking employment."

"That maybe so, but I still think she is not too proud to work," Mary replied, indignantly. "What about Sunday school?" she added with hope.

"The teachers are volunteers, they don't get paid," Albert said with regret.

"Oh, I see, of course not, silly me." Mary sounded despondent.

"Can her husband's family not help her?" Albert enquired.

"They live on the mainland; they have nothing to do with her. Apparently, they didn't agree with their son marrying a British woman and then eloping to Tenerife. They never forgave her for luring him away, that's what they believe, but of course it was not true, as Dorothy pointed out, it was her husband's wish to live in Tenerife, she wanted to live in England. But she sees Tenerife as her home now and really doesn't want to have to return to England."

"I see." Albert checked his watch; he had a sick parishioner he had promised to check in on after the service and he was now running late. "Leave it with me, Mary—let me have a think. And Mary, try not to worry. I'm sure we will work something out."

Mary nodded. "Yes, I know. I just wish I could help."

"The Lord will provide, HE always does." He smiled broadly and accompanied Mary out of the door. She thanked him and then left. Albert pulled out a large brass key from his trouser pocket, locked the door and walked briskly down the street, thinking about Dorothy and how he could help her. As expatriates living on the island together, so far away from home and as good Christians, they needed to support and help each other through difficult times.

The clouds had started to gather, as if stuck on top of Mount Teide, lingering, and spreading far and wide over the north of the island, a common occurrence in Puerto De La Cruz, but the air still felt warm and humid. Esperanza removed her shoes and then sat down on the harbour wall, letting her feet dangle loosely below. It was a place she often came to for inspiration while watching the fishing boats toing and froing. The sea was always calmer here, it had a peaceful feel, despite many people passing by, including fisherwomen calling out the day's catch that their husbands had brought in earlier that morning. Being close to the sea somehow made her feel close to her father. Her long dark hair was scraped neatly back in a tight bun with a yellow hibiscus loosely poking through, matching the colour of her dress. She had picked it on her walk down to the harbour, hoping it would stay, so far, it had. Her stomach gave an impertinent growl, and she placed the palm of her hand on top, to silence it. She had eaten one slice of bread with jam early that morning but now it was late afternoon. Lunch was no longer affordable in the Rodriguez' household. *We need to tighten our purse strings, and you girls will be out foraging soon,* Dorothy, had warned Esperanza and her sisters. Esperanza pulled a small notepad and pencil from her pocket. The inspiration had suddenly come to her and so she began to scribble.

The perfume of the sea engulfed them. The wind had become an orchestral conductor of the waves, lashing... She paused, looked at the sea. It was still calm, but towards San Telmo it was a different story, the waves would undoubtedly have been lashing, or perhaps cascading, and so she continued with that image firmly in her mind. *Waves lashing... cascading over the rocks, crashing like thunder and ...*

She looked up and turned her head in

thought, casting her eyes on a rather handsome boy that had appeared as if from nowhere, carrying a bucket in one hand and a fishing rod in the other. He turned, facing her direction. She quickly looked the other way, feeling her face becoming warm with embarrassment. He was like a character from one of her stories—dark hair, dark eyes, muscular physique. She never paid much attention to boys, they were annoying, difficult to speak to and the local boys were nothing to look at either in her opinion, but he was different, he was definitely different.

She reread the line she had just written but the words had gone again. Tapping the pencil on her bottom lip in thought she couldn't help but turn her head to check if he was still there. He was. He reeled in the fishing rod with ease, despite it being a large catch. Oh goodness he had caught a whopper! She stared in awe. He looked so strong and confident. She guessed him to be close to her own age of seventeen years or possibly a little older. Yes, now she had studied him a little more, perhaps he was nineteen maybe even twenty. Why had she never seen him before?

A moment later he picked up the bucket and was heading her way. Her nerves got the better of her. She dropped her pencil and the quickly grabbed it from the wall, crossing out what she had just written and then writing the same words again and again to display the action of being busy.

A bucket placed heavily on the wall next to her shoes, forced her gaze upwards. It was *him!*

"Hola." He gave a friendly smile. "Do you mind?" he asked, speaking in Spanish with a strong Canarian accent. He pointed to the spot next to her on the wall. She nodded in agreement, trying to contain her nerves, and hoping her cheeks had not turned too crimson. A strong whiff of fish hit her nostrils. She peered into the bucket that was at her side.

"It's alright, it is dead," he smirked and then she giggled.

"Esperanza Rodgriguez, pleased to meet you!" She stretched out her hand. Her mother had always taught her good manners in a typically British fashion.

"Carlos Garcia," he accepted her handshake but finding it a little awkward, he leaned forward and kissed her on both cheeks instead, in the normal local customary way.

His closeness sent quivers down her spine. She didn't care about the pong of the fish or the fact that he was a little sweaty. None of that mattered at all, he was incredibly handsome and even more so up close. She faced the sea to try and gain her composure.

"Where are you from?" He noticed her accent wasn't local. He watched her as she moved her bare feet back and forth in rhythm to the sea lapping at the shore below them.

"I was born on the mainland—Malaga. My

father was Spanish, my mother is English."

"Was Spanish—so has your father...?

"Yes, he passed away five years ago at sea in a boating accident." Speaking about it was still so painful. She could see in her mind's eye her mother, distraught, crying hysterically at the news that he had been killed on that fateful night.

"And your mother? Sorry I'm asking too many questions."

"No, it's fine. My mother is well, and I have two younger sisters. Anyway, what about you? I've never seen you here before."

"I'm from La Gomera." He pointed in the direction of the island across the water, although it was too far away to see from where they were sitting. "Do you know La Gomera?"

His question made her giggle. "Yes, I know La Gomera."

"Of course you do, you are educated, I can see that."

"I've not been there though. I just know where it is," she said in attempt to make him feel less of a fool for asking her if she knew where it was.

He looked pensively out towards the sea. "I wish for better things in my life," he sighed.

Esperanza chuckled. "Don't we all?"

"I'm not educated like you. My father is a farmer, my grandfather was a farmer, his father too and it's expected for me to be the same—growing wheat, legumes, potatoes, fruit—all so very exciting!" He rolled his deep brown eyes.

"You might find something better one day. I want to be an author." She beamed at the idea.

He noticed how pretty she was, especially when she smiled. He looked down at the notepad and pencil at her side.

She grabbed it before he had a chance to pick it up. "It's not finished yet; in fact I've hardly written anything—it's just some ideas." She blushed profusely.

He decided not to push her on it, he couldn't read anyway.

"Carlos!" A man in the distance called out to him, followed by a whistle, signalling for his return.

"That's my father, we need to go home now."

"Oh, I see." She tried her best to hide her disappointment. "Well, it was very nice to meet you."

He could sense her sadness.

"I come here once a week now my father is selling in Tenerife."

Her face lit up. "Maybe I will see you next week then."

He jumped to his feet and picked up his fishing rod. "Maybe you will. Bring some of your writing and you can read it to me."

"Maybe," she replied, looking coy.

He flashed that handsome smile of his that would make any girl's heart melt and then he ran off.

Esperanza watched his retreating back.

Standing up for a better look, she could see him getting into a boat with his father. It was a small, modest boat, typical of the types of boats that were used for island hopping. There were many like that coming back and forth into the harbour of Puerto De La Cruz. She smiled broadly, excited to see him again next week, she could hardly wait. Her stomach suddenly gave another impatient growl. Thank goodness it had not done that while he had been sitting next to her. She turned to find her shoes and then spotted the bucket with the fish. "Oh no! She looked over to see if he was still there, but the boat had already left the shore. She peered into the bucket. What was she to do with a fish? She couldn't keep it until next week, it would stink by then. The best thing to do would be to take it home she decided. It would make an excellent supper, mother would be delighted, and she could give back the bucket next week. A good reason to see him again. Not that she really needed a reason as such, not now that they were acquainted. He seemed to enjoy speaking with her as much as she did him.

The heat of the late afternoon sunshine had burnt away the clouds as Esperanza ran home, not wanting the fish to get any warmer than it was. Slightly out of breath, she reached the brightly painted blue townhouse —the Rodriguez's home. It was a typical Canarian property with two wooden balconies, located off each of the upstairs rooms. Handcraft wooden structures were a sign of wealth. The house looked both expensive and homely. It was no wonder Dorothy feared losing their home if she couldn't find a solution to their dwindling funds. It was in close proximity to the centre of Puerto De La Cruz making it an even more desirable property, but Dorothy didn't want to sell it unless it was absolutely necessary.

"Mama!" Passing through the main reception room, opulently furnished with sumptuous seating and an open log fireplace, she dashed into the back room to find her mother spooning jam into jars on the old oak wooden table that was the focal point of the kitchen. The wooden beams made the room look smaller than it was and a little dark, but that was the idea, to keep it cool during the long hot summers.

Dorothy looked up, wiping her hands on her apron. "I was starting to think you had left home. Where have you been? I could have done with your help picking berries to make this jam." She looked tired, dark lines encompassed her hazel eyes, owing to her lack of sleep, worrying about her finances. Yet, despite this, Dorothy looked younger than her forty-three years, she was an attractive, women, tall, slim with hair the colour of chestnut.

"I've brought us supper." Esperanza smiled proudly, placing the bucket onto the table in front of her to see.

She peered into the bucket, not knowing

what to expect, least of all a fish, and gasped with surprise.

"It's a big fish," Esperanza said, still smiling.

"Yes, I can see that." She eyed her daughter suspiciously. "How did you... You didn't steal it from the fishing boats?"

"No! Of course not." Esperanza looked insulted.

"Then where did it come from?"

"I found it."

Dorothy's eyebrows knitted together in a deep frown. "Found it where?"

"Down at the harbour, on the wall."

"Then it obviously belongs to one of the fishermen. You can't just go around poaching their catch, pardon the expression!" Dorothy stood with her hands firmly on her hips as she always did when she got annoyed. "My goodness what will they think if they find out? We are a well-respected family on this island."

Esperanza decided to come clean and explain. "No, you don't understand. I know who the fish belongs to. He forgot it, you see, and he doesn't live here in Puerto."

This was sounding worse by the minute. Dorothy listened with a pained, confused expression. "Well, where does he live? And who is *he*?"

"His name is Carlos Garcia, and he lives in La Gomera."

"La Gomera?"

"Yes, the island La Gomera, his father was

selling produce from their farm and Carlos was fishing while he was waiting for him." She rattled on hardly pausing for breath. "We started talking and then his father called him, and then he ran off and forgot the fish. He won't be back until next week. We can't keep it for him, it'll go bad," she said matter of fact.

"I see. Well, I don't feel comfortable about eating his fish, but, as you say, we can't keep it until next week, can we?" A small smile crept across Dorothy's face. "I've got some potatoes in the pantry and a few carrots and if you go and pick a couple of lemons from the garden to go with the fish, I'll make us a feast fit for a king!" Dorothy's eyes gleamed, thankful that supper was now sorted and a hearty one at that.

Esperanza grinned happily, she couldn't wait, she was starving.

"And Espe, check on your sisters in the back room, they should be reading."

"Yes, Mama."

"Oh, and one more thing."

Esperanza turned to face her mother again. "You really shouldn't be speaking to young men, especially from another island." *And particularly a farmer's son* but she didn't dare say that part. Not that she had anything against farmers, but she was unsure of the boy's intentions and if a romance should blossom, she had hoped for much better for her daughter than to be married to a farmer from La Gomera.

51

Esperanza nodded reluctantly. "I should give him his bucket though, shouldn't I?" She asked in hope.

"Of course," Dorothy agreed. "That would be good manners and you should also apologise and then thank him for the fish, even though he didn't exactly give it to you." She inspected the fish in the bucket again. It was certainly a good size and would feed them for at least two dinners. Her prayers at church that morning had been answered, well at least for tonight and tomorrow anyway!

"Yes, Mama," Esperanza nodded then went off in search for her sisters.

Chapter Five

The black urn was placed on the shelf next to Grace's photo in the living room. The last couple of days had been a whirlwind for Jen, a roller coaster of emotions and she was certain she would never have got through it, had it have not been for Mrs Schneider. It wasn't only the shock of seeing Grace laid out in a box and then the cremation, but the trip to Grace's lawyers office that morning had knocked her for six.

She walked into the kitchen, poured herself a glass of rose from the fridge and then went out to sit in the garden. Clouds rolled in from the sea and the air felt warm and muggy. What was she to do? Grace had now given her an opportunity to make a big change in her life, but would she be brave enough to take it? Her thoughts were disturbed by the intrusive ring of her mobile phone. She fished it out of her pocket. Kate's name flashed up on the screen and she answered.

"Hey! How are you holding up?" Kate's friendly voice echoed down the line, offering comfort.

"Oh Kate, I don't even know where to start."

"I can imagine it must have been tough."

"Saying goodbye to Grace, yes, it was tough. I brought the ashes back here to the villa, I don't know what to do with them, I haven't decided yet," she sighed. "I'm faced with another big decision."

"Go on," Kate replied, intrigued.

"Grace left a will," Jen continued. "She left me this villa."

"Oh my goodness, really?"

"And that's not all. She left me her savings too—sixty-two thousand euros of them."

"Sixty-two thousand! My God, Jen!"

"I know, I can't believe it. My head is all over the place." She paused, took a sip of wine and sighed again. "I think this could be life changing, Kate."

"Well, a villa and sixty-two thousand euros is pretty big, it means free holidays and plenty of spending money, or are you going to sell it? It could bring you quite a tidy sum on top of what she has left you?"

"No, I couldn't possibly sell this place, it was Grace's home, her pride and joy." Jen glided her toes through the softness of the grass beneath her. "It's a special place, Kate. I can't sell it."

"Then your holidays for life are sorted, and mine too," she chuckled down the phone.

"I'm not thinking of it as a holiday home, although you would always be welcome. Kate, I think I want to live here."

Kate almost dropped the phone. "Jen, you can't be serious? What about David, your job? Your life here in England?"

"What life? I have a husband who doesn't even notice me, in fact, I've had one text message since I've been here and that was because he was searching for his navy-blue tie and couldn't find it. Alison has her own life and I'm sure she would love coming out here for holidays. And as for my job, I'm tired of teaching, I need a change."

"Wow! When you put it like that… but are you sure it's not the grief talking?"

"I have to think things through properly, admittedly, I know that, but no I don't think it's the grief, I think Grace's death is my wake-up call. I'm due to fly back to England on Saturday and my heart sinks at the very idea. I just don't want to leave. I don't want to go back to my old life."

Kate gave a short snort of a laugh down the phone. "God, neither would I if I had a lovely villa and all that money out there."

Jen smiled wryly. "I'm not going to be splashing the cash. I need to think about what I will do with it." She checked her watch, it was 5.30pm. "Kate, I have to go and get something to eat, I haven't eaten all day. Can I call you later?"

"Yes sure, you know you can call me any time."

"Thanks, and please don't say a word to anyone until I figure this all out."

"Mum's the word! I'm truly excited for you, although I'll miss you if you moved over there."

"And I'd miss you too but I'm only a plane ride away."

They hung up and Jen gave a big sigh. Speaking about the idea of living in Tenerife somehow seemed to make it more real. She hadn't mentioned it to the lawyer or Mrs Schneider, Kate was the first person she had told, and it felt like a weight off her shoulders sharing her thoughts.

She padded barefoot across the cool tiles on the kitchen floor, checked the fridge and then the cupboard for something to eat. There were eggs, pasta, and a few other ingredients that could be whisked into something substantial, but she wasn't in the mood for cooking and had a much better idea instead. There were lots of lovely little restaurants nearby, it was time for her to get out and relax a bit after the past stressful and eventful few days.

She went into the bedroom, changed her top, nipped into the bathroom and gave her armpits a quick squirt of deodorant and then flicked a comb through her curls before applying a little bit of soft pink lipstick, which happened to match her top. Wearing tight jeans, a pair of silver sandals with her hair loosely cascading down her back, she looked and felt youthful again despite the recent strain she had been under. She closed the terrace doors and grabbed her keys next to the front door. A moment later she was wandering down the narrow street lined with sweet smelling bougainvillea hanging over the many walls of whitewashed villas. She inhaled the air, for first time in as long as she could remember she felt alive. And with a spring in her step, she had no idea why suddenly she felt as free as a bird. Had she made her decision to stay? Could she really start a new life without David? Thanks to Grace, she now had a home, a beautiful home at that, and even enough money to maybe set up a new business, although what business she had no idea, not a clue. Her mind was buzzing.

She reached the end of the road and suddenly stopped, mesmerised by the little church standing before her. And without realising, she found herself walking up the steps towards it. Above the arched threshold it read *Parroquia De San Amaro. Siglo XVI.* She shivered despite the warm breeze. Not being able to stop herself, she walked inside. It was the smallest church she had ever seen, not that she went to church as a rule, other than weddings, funerals, and christenings. Drawn to the elaborate filigree alter, she stood before it, staring in awe. A tide of sadness washed over her. Was it because of losing Grace? No. It felt different than the grief she had felt for Grace, more like a deep sadness from the past, something she couldn't quite recall, something linked to this pretty little church. But that would be impossible, she had never even been inside this church until now. She shivered again and this time the air grew colder. The hairs on the back of her neck prickled as did the hairs on her arms. With glazed eyes from her tears, she noticed an image forming before her at the alter. The back of a young woman in a long, white, wedding dress, kneeling— beside her, a man dressed in a suit. Jen could feel in her own heart the woman's terrible pain and emptiness, a deep penetrating sadness. This was not a marriage born out of love and happiness. She blinked hard, the tears now stinging her eyes forced her to grab a tissue from her handbag and dab them. When she looked up again the vision had disappeared. Not understanding anything about what had just happened, she turned away from the alter and took a moment to regain her composure. Whatever had happened, whatever she saw, it had not been like anything she had ever experienced before in her life and she didn't know if it was a sign, perhaps God's way or sending a message to her about her own life and her own marriage?

To her right, she spotted a candle box. Inspecting it closely, she fathomed how it worked, took out a coin from her handbag and thrust it into the small wooden slot. Immediately a candle lit. She spoke quietly, her voice barely more than an audible whisper.

"For you Grace. Rest in peace. I miss you. Oh, and thank you. I promise to look after your home and make good use of the money." She smiled fondly, drifting a finger softly along the candle box. The artificial candle flickered and then stabilized.

By the time Jen stepped out of the church, the sun had set, and the streetlamps were turning on. Taking a left turn, she followed a little street dotted with cafes and restaurants and then stopped to read the menu board from one of them. Its name above the door read *"Casa De Pedro."* The menu was written in Spanish with a picture below to show what each dish was. There was also a host of tapas she liked the look of and the aroma coming from inside was inviting. The waiter spotted her and pointed to an available table on the covered terrace. She smiled and walked inside.

"Is this OK for you, or if you are feeling cold, perhaps a table inside?" Inside was terribly busy and so she accepted a quiet table outside, finding it amusing that he should find it cold. He handed her the menu.

"No, it's not cold," she grinned. "I come from England; it is very cold there, but not here."

He gave a short laugh. "For us locals, anything less than twenty degrees is cold."

She accepted the menu. "Then I would advise you not to visit England in the winter."

"I did once. I went to London in February. *Madre Mia, frio,* so cold!" He gave a dramatized shake of his entire body, making Jen laugh.

"What can I get you to drink?" His note pad and pen were poised ready to take her order.

"Glass of red wine, Rioja, please."

"Wonderful." He was gone in a flash leaving her to mull over the menu.

A group of men stood at the bar chatting animatedly about anything and everything but in particular politics, waving their hands around and getting louder by the minute. To Jen it sounded like a heated discussion, she couldn't understand a word they were saying. Little did she know that it was perfectly normal for the locals to speak loudly when they got excited, be it good or bad.

The waiter returned. He placed a new white, paper cloth on the table and cutlery, and a basket of freshly cut baguette. Jen then ordered a variety of tapas, and once again the waiter was off attending to her order. She watched his retreating back lost in thought about how different life was here, how relaxed it was, and how people seemed to really live and enjoy life to the full. They weren't existing from day to day caught in the rat race of building careers like she had been for many years. They worked to live, not lived to work. They had the right attitude and that inspired Jen far more than the life she had been leading.

One of the men standing at the bar, dressed in a brown leather jacket, and dark blue jeans, caught her eye, he smiled at her. She suddenly realised she must have been staring right through him lost in her thoughts. Embarrassed, she returned his smile politely and looked the other way.

There was so much to think about. She would have to return to the UK at some point to collect her things. Would David even care about her leaving him, she wondered. Would he make a fuss about it, argue, expect them to tear strips out of each other and then try and save their marriage? - she hoped not, she didn't have the energy, or care enough to do that. Their marriage died so long ago, she couldn't even recall the last time they had made love, it was that long. Then there was Alison, how would she take the news of her mum and dad splitting up and her mum moving abroad? The thought of telling Alison immediately made her nervous. She took a large swig of wine to calm herself. Best not think about that right now at this moment. The waiter placed an array of colourful tapas on the table, taking her mind off things.

"Enjoy!" he said, before leaving her to dig in. They smelt delicious. She tried the meatballs in tomato sauce first, known by the locals as *albondigas*. They tasted even better than they smelt, rich in garlic and herbs.

The group of men at the bar paid and then spilled onto the terrace, squeezing through the tables as they made their way out. With a loud smash of a glass, the man wearing a brown leather jacket immediately turned around and realised he had knocked Jen's glass of wine to the floor.

"Perdon! Sorry!"

"It's OK," Jen flashed a reassuring smile.

"Let me buy you another one." Before she could answer, he called out to the waiter and asked for a replacement. The waiter rushed over and started clearing up broken glass and red wine that had spilt on the empty chair beside her, straight to the floor.

Jen felt a little embarrassed. "Really, there's no need, accidents happen."

"Yes of course there is need." He grinned, displaying a row of pearly white teeth. He was handsome, there was no denying that. And if he wanted to replace her drink he had knocked over, then why not?

"Thank you," she replied graciously.

"You like Papas Arrugadas?"

"Sorry?" She had no idea what he had just said.

He pointed to the potatoes she had not got around to eating yet. "How you say it? Um potatoes with wrinkles." They both laughed.

"Yes, I love potatoes with wrinkles."

"It's a typical Canarian dish. Are you on holiday?" He glanced over at his friends who were waiting patiently on the pavement for him and then he looked back at Jen expectantly for her answer.

"Not exactly. It's a long story." A wave of sadness came over her, which didn't go unnoticed.

"Sorry I didn't mean..."

"No, it's fine."

The waiter placed a large glass of wine on the table for her. She thanked him and turned her attention back to the handsome man in front of her. "I think I'm going to be living here," she said, taking herself by surprise.

"Oh," he seemed equally as surprised and, also happy about it, although he had no idea why. "Well, I'm pleased to meet you," he said.

His English was very good, Jen noticed.

"And you, too. I'm Jennifer Williams," she said using her maiden name, not wishing to acknowledge her married name. "But everyone calls me Jen." She shrugged her shoulders.

He laughed. "I'm Carlos Garcia and everyone calls me Carlos, that's when they are being nice," he shrugged his shoulders too. Again, they laughed.

"It was my father's name; my grandfather's name and it is also my son's name."

"That must be confusing at family parties," Jen giggled.

"Yes, it can be, although my grandfather has now passed away. My father we call Pops, and we call my son Carlito. It means little Carlos."

"I see." She had no idea why she felt

disappointed that he used the word "we" referring to probably himself and his wife, or maybe he was referring to his family in general. Of course he would be married, he was too handsome and charming not to be. And she was married too, although it didn't feel like it and probably wouldn't be for much longer, not that she had any interest in looking for a new relationship, far from it.

"Venga, Carlos!" one of the men called out from the street, now getting impatient, telling him to hurry up.

He looked at her apologetically. "Sorry, I must go."

"Yes of course. And thank you for the wine."

"My pleasure, sorry I knocked it over." He flashed that incredible smile of his again and then left.

If only Grace had been there to see this, she would have ridiculed her all night, a good-looking Canarian buying her a drink, she could hear Grace's squawky laugh, the one she always did when she got excited. *Carlos Garcia,* she whispered under her breath with a small smile.

Chapter Six

"Carlos!" Esperanza felt her stomach churn with excitement as she ran towards him along the harbour wall, holding the blue bucket firmly in her hand. He was fishing and this time had a red bucket at his side.

"Hola!" She greeted him, slightly out of breath.

"So that's what happened to my bucket," he said, pointing to it with a frown creasing his forehead. "I suppose you ate my fish too."

"Um, well, you forgot it." Esperanza appeared flustered, and he was enjoying every moment of playfully teasing her.

"And so you thought it would be alright to eat my fish? I worked hard to catch it. We had to go hungry that night."

"I called out to you and you were gone. What was I supposed to do? I'm sorry you went hungry."

She looked close to tears, so he thought he should call an end to her torment and he burst out laughing.

Realising he was teasing her; she playfully hit his arm and then removed her shoes and sat down next to him on the wall.

"Was it tasty—my fish?" he asked, smiling from his eyes.

"Delicious." A look of worry appeared on her face again. "Did you really go hungry that night?"

He laughed at her innocence. "I live on a farm; we never go hungry." He gave her a sideways nudge noticing her pretty cornflower dress. "I'm guessing you never go hungry either."

"Me? No of course not," she lied, not wishing to disclose the family secret that they had next to no money and she was hungry most of the time these days.

"Oh, here we go." He jumped to his feet, taking her by surprise. "I think I've caught one!" He started reeling it in and a moment later a medium sized sea bream wriggled vigorously from the end of the line. He turned to face her, beaming with pride.

"You are good at fishing," she said, happy for him.

He placed the fish in the bucket then took out more tackle to add to the end of the line. "Nothing to it. Your turn. Stand up." He thrust the fishing rod in her hands, then stood behind her, cupping his hands over hers to steady her grip of the rod. She could feel the warmth of his breath on her cheek and the heat of his body against hers as he guided her slowly. It felt seductive and sensuous, her whole body quivered with delight.

"Now we pull it up and throw it out." The line ended up in the water somewhere in the distance. "You can sit down now; it could be a while."

She did as he said and sat down, he followed suit next to her. "Did you bring your story to read to me?"

She was surprised he remembered. "No, I've not finished writing it and it's not very good."

"Says who?"

"Me, I say it is not."

"I'm sure it is and if you want to be a published author one day, you are going to have to let others be the judge if it's good or not."

Esperanza nodded in agreement, she knew he was right, but she lacked confidence in letting anyone read her work, something she would have to get over one day as Carlos rightly pointed out.

"I know but..." She was interrupted by a tug on the fishing rod. "Oh, I felt something! I think I've caught a fish!" She jumped up excitedly.

"Alright, softly," he instructed standing closely at her side, intrigued as she was to see how big it was. And it was another sea bream, quite a good size too. Carlos clenched it hard and unhooked the fish before throwing it into the blue bucket next to them. "That one is yours."

"No, I couldn't, really? I mean it's bigger than the one you caught."

"Are you bragging now?" He teased her again. She smiled coyly; she was getting used to his sense of humour. "No, I'm not bragging. I couldn't have done it without you."

"You caught it, it's yours. I'll get my bucket back next week," he grinned.

She had no idea how she would explain a second fish to her mother, but at least supper was sorted for another two nights.

They sat for a while longer on the wall, chatting, giggling about anything that sprung to mind and eventually when Carlos' father appeared in the distance, calling him back, Esperanza felt a pang of regret at having to say goodbye to him for another week. But at least she knew she would see him again, and she could use the excuse of returning his bucket, if her mother should ask, which she probably would.

The sky was dark grey, and the wind had picked up as Esperanza made her way back home. She rehearsed in her head different ways of explaining how she obtained yet another fish. And then, taking her by surprise, the heavens opened to a torrential down pour, so much so that she could hardly see the street opposite her. She ran as fast she could for shelter, but the cobbles were slippery. And as she took the next corner, she slipped and fell to the ground, hitting her head hard, blood immediately spilled from beneath her. As if someone had just turned out the lights, everything went black.

Jen stirred in her sleep, her eyelids fluttering as she muttered something inaudible. The dark silhouette hovered next to the curtains that were swaying softly in the cool breeze. Jen's eyes fluttered again and then opened. Sleepily she turned her head towards the window, squinting. Was that a woman dressed in black or her sleepy eyes playing tricks? Feeling uneasy, she reached out with a trembling hand and clicked the bedside lamp. Nothing. No woman, only the curtains dancing back and forth in the wind. She sighed with relief, feeling silly for thinking anything so bizarre.

Stepping out of bed, wincing at the sting of the cold tiled floor beneath her feet, she closed the window tightly, before getting back into bed. She checked the time on her watch—4am. Sighing wearily she snuggled back under the sheets and closed her eyes again.

It was 9.05am when Jen woke again. Looking at her watch, she was horrified that she had slept that long. In England she was always up around 7.30am, even at weekends but this past week had really taken its toll and she obviously needed her rest.

Pulling herself out of bed, she pushed her feet into her slippers and stood up, stretching her arms high and giving a yawn. Immediately her thoughts turned to the evening before and Carlos Garcia. She trotted off to the bathroom, chiding herself for thinking about him again. She couldn't get rid of the image of his face and his charming smile that had popped into her head. He was just a man who knocked over her glass by accident and bought her a drink. Get over it Jen, stop thinking about him like a love struck teenager! She had far more important things to think about like...

"Oh my goodness not again! What is your obsession with this bathroom?" The speckled green gecko stared back at her with its big dark eyes from the wall next to the toilet. "Come on, move." She prodded it with a piece of toilet roll wrapped around her finger, not wishing to touch it with her bare hands, trying to usher it towards the tiny window that she had forgotten to close the night before. This time the gecko was not having any of it and shot off in another direction. She was bursting to go to the loo and really couldn't be doing with the hassle, so she sat down on the toilet, as it crossed her path and left the bathroom, heading off down the hallway. By the time she had finished her business, flushed the toilet, washed her hands, and went in search for it, it was nowhere to be seen.

The morning sunlight shone brightly through the glass doors filling the kitchen with warmth. Jen, placing the kettle under the tap, felt a flood of happiness, like this was the first day of her new life. She had made the decision last night not to go back to England. Villa Esperanza was her new home now. She had text David, emailed work, and then turned off her phone.

She made herself a cup of coffee, buttered a croissant that she had picked up from the bakery yesterday, smothered it with strawberry jam, then took her breakfast outside to eat it in the garden.

The warm air hit her, stepping outside in her silk pajamas and slippers. It was hard to believe it was winter. The only reminder was Mount Teide's peak covered in snow. She sat down at the table, enjoying the sunshine on her skin while admiring the garden. The grass would need cutting soon and she wondered where Grace kept the lawnmower or perhaps she had a gardener.

After finishing the last mouthful of her croissant, she decided to face the music and go and find her mobile phone, time to face the consequences of her actions from the night before. School, without a doubt, wouldn't be happy about her not working her notice.

She found her phone laying on the coffee table, in the living room. As she reached down to pick it up, she heard the kettle boiling in the kitchen. Dashing back through to the kitchen with her phone in her hand, she stood for a moment watching the steam rise into the air. Maybe it had an electrical fault. It could be dangerous she decided and quickly unplugged it, making a mental note to pick up a new one later today when she went into town.

Returning to her chair in the garden, she waited for her phone to load and then the messages started, one after the other. Eight missed calls from David, one message from Kate asking her to call her when she could and a sweet text from Alison asking if she was OK? Oh gosh, Alison, she needed to call her today and tell her what was going on. She felt a terrible mother for not calling her last night, what if David told her before she had a chance to? She didn't want Alison thinking she was abandoning her. The loud ring of her phone made her almost jump out of her skin. Seeing David's name on the screen, she hesitated. She knew she couldn't avoid him forever, better get this over with now and then she could get on with her day.

"Hello," she answered sheepishly, like a child who knew she was about to be told off. And she was correct. He was fuming.

"Oh, finally you turn your phone on. What in God's name are you thinking?" His voice bellowed down the line. "You send me a message late at night to say you've inherited a villa in...." he cursed, spitting his words. "...Tenerife," he continued. "And you are not coming back!"

He rarely used the 'f' word, so she knew he was extremely upset or incredibly angry that he had lost her now, that their marriage was finally over, and she had been the one to end it.

"Yes, I probably shouldn't have text you," she grimaced biting her bottom lip.

"Oh, you think?"

"It's all happened so quickly; I'm still trying to get my head around things."

"Yes, which means it is a rash decision that needs to be talked through—face to face." He ran his fingers though his uncombed hair, sitting at the breakfast table in front of a cup of tea that was now cold. He had called in sick after not sleeping all night.

"There's nothing really to talk about," she replied calmly. "Things have not been good between us for a long time, David. You know that. You are married to the bank, not me."

"Oh, so it's my fault, is it? I take my career seriously, I work hard to give you and Alison a nice home, pay for her university and now you repay me by leaving me... after twenty-three years of marriage!"

"No, it's not like that and you know it. Yes, you work hard. I know you care about Alison, when you have time for her but..."

"What's that supposed to mean, when I have time?"

"You never came home before 7pm all throughout her childhood and most nights you were back out again by 8pm. She got a quick kiss goodnight, and you were off."

"I spent time with her, with you both, at the weekends," he replied, sounding highly insulted.

"You took Alison horse riding every Sunday, even though she didn't want to go and you spent Saturday nights with your head in a book when we were supposed to be watching a movie together. And whenever I suggested going out, you always said you didn't feel like it."

"I was tired from working long hours all week. And of course Alison liked horse riding."

"See that's the problem, you don't listen, she told you many times she didn't. You never listen to Alison and you never listen to me. You do what you want—when you want and to hell with anyone else. Well, this time it's my turn. I've had enough of being in a stale boring relationship. I want out, David."

Realising he was losing his fight with her; it was time to change tactic. "I'm sorry Jen. OK, maybe I haven't been the best of husbands or father—maybe I should have spent more time with you both—I was busy trying to build a career and to earn money for us to have a nice life together as a family.

"Only that didn't happen, did it, David? You may have earned the money but that's as far as it goes—as for a nice life..."

"We can work this out. Come back home. We don't have to move to Bournemouth, I can turn down the promotion. Just come home." He sounded close to tears which took her by surprise.

"It's not my home anymore. It stopped being home when Alison left. And you don't have to turn down the promotion for me," she said, knowing full well that he wouldn't, it was just a way of coaxing her back.

"Can't we at least try and work through this? For Alison's sake?" He knew he was clutching at straws now.

"Alison is a grown woman; she doesn't need us to be together. She needs her parents to be happy and if they can't be happy together, then at least they can be apart.

A knock on the glass patio doors behind her, forced Jen to turn around. Mrs Schneider stood in the doorway with a freshly baked loaf of bread in her hands. The aroma wafted into the kitchen.

Jen smiled and ushered her inside. "David, I'm going to have to go now."

"What? No...We need to speak."

"I think we have said everything," she said coolly and then hung up.

"Mrs Schneider." Jen smiled, trying to put any thoughts of David to the back of her mind.

"I made two loaves of bread and one is for

you." She held out the bread for her to take.

"Thank you, smells delicious."

"I suppose you will be going back to England soon?" Mrs Schneider enquired watching her closely as she placed the loaf on the wooden chopping board. Jen's phone rang again, and she instantly turned it off.

Mrs Schneider noticed the troubled look in her eyes. "I know it's none of my business but if you need someone to talk to."

Without warning Jen burst into tears, surprising not just Mrs Schneider but herself too. Yesterday she had felt so happy and today she didn't know what she felt anymore. Guilty for leaving David and for thinking of herself for once, guilty for wanting to move on with her life without him. Maybe she was having a midlife crisis, nothing made sense.

"Come now. *Alles Gut.*" She hugged Jen tightly. When Jen finally stopped crying, Mrs Schneider said, "sit down in the garden, I'll make us some coffee." Jen nodded and went off to sit down outside. A couple of minutes later, Mrs Schneider arrived with two cups of steaming coffee. "Do you take sugar?"

Jen shook her head. "No thank you. I'm sorry for blubbering all over you. Look at me, I'm a mess." She pointed at her pajamas. "I'm not even dressed at this hour."

"Quatsch!—rubbish as you English say. You've been through a difficult time. I miss Grace too."

A tear trickled down Jen's cheek, guilty again that she wasn't crying over Grace but herself, for her lack of feelings for David, her own confused feelings about moving to Tenerife and starting a new life. "It's more than that," she confessed before taking a sip of coffee. "I've left my husband."

"Oh, I see." Mrs Schneider looked taken a back.

"Things have not been good between us for a lot of years. I think I only stayed for as long as I did because of our daughter. Now Alison is at university there's no reason for me to stay anymore."

"I understand." She tapped her hand affectionately. "But what are you going to do? Where are you going to go?"

"Here, stay here. Well at least I thought I was until I spoke to David just then and, well, now I don't know if I'm just being stupid or selfish, or both."

Mrs Schneider frowned. "You are neither stupid nor selfish. You are in an unhappy marriage and have spent years that way, putting your daughter first. You are far from selfish and deciding to leave is by no means stupid."

Jen's lips curled into a grateful smile. "I'm lucky to have you, Mrs Schneider."

"Jen, please, no more calling me Mrs Schneider. We are friends now, please call me Petra. I never understood why Grace didn't call me Petra, Mrs Schneider sounds so formal,"

Jen chuckled. "OK, Petra it is from now on, I promise."

"And do you also promise that you will put yourself first from now on?" If we have both learned anything recently—and that is, life is too short. You must live it and do what you want. You will not get these years back, trust me when I say you will soon be as old as I."

Jen pushed back her shoulders against the back of the chair. "You are right, Mrs...Petra. You are absolutely right! And for the record, you are not old. One is only as old as one feels."

"Then I am ancient," Petra chuckled.

Chapter Seven

They ran in different directions, taking shelter from the rain. No one had even noticed poor Esperanza sprawled out on the roadside, blood trickling from behind her head and her gashed left knee, that also oozed onto the concrete beneath her. A grey, mangy looking dog, soaked to the skin, ran towards Esperanza. It stopped to sniff her hair and gave a sympathetic whine, but the scent of the fish on the other side of the road, next to the bucket, having been thrown out by the force from Esperanza's fall, caught its attention and it headed in that direction. It gave a quick appreciative lick to the fish and then clenched it firmly between its jaws before making off in haste.

Albert Jones glanced at his watch. If this rain did not subside soon, he would be late for the 6.30pm prayer service. He hovered in the doorway of a closed down tavern. His mind wandered to Dorothy and how he might be able to help her. Perhaps she could organize a jumble sale in the church grounds and if enough was sold, he could pay her some money for her trouble. Or maybe a cake sale. He pondered which one would be more profitable, but then his eyes fell on what looked like someone laying by the roadside in the distance. He squinted through his spectacles. Gosh it certainly looked like a person. Forgetting about the rain which had fortunately slowed down now anyway, he dashed up the road and was horrified to see it was Dorothy's daughter.

"Esperanza!" He tapped her face gently. She moved her head slightly, groaned, then opened her eyes, recognizing the blurry outline of Albert in front of her.

"Vicar."

Her voice was hoarse, and he could see she was in a lot of pain.

"Yes. Don't worry, I'm going to help you." He took off his jacket, rolled it up, lifted her head and slid it under to make her more comfortable. Fortunately, the heavy bleeding from her head had now stopped. He took a closer look, the wound was not big, but she had lost a lot of blood, noticing the size of the sticky pool next to her. He glanced down at her knee. It was still bleeding and seemed deep. He reached for his handkerchief and applied pressure to it to try and stop the bleeding.

"My fish." Esperanza said, regaining her voice properly now. Her head was throbbing, and her knee was stinging. She struggled to remember what had happened and why she was laying in the road in such a state.

"Fish?" Albert peered at her from over his spectacles that had fallen halfway down his nose. Was she hallucinating? He needed to get her to a doctor and quickly.

"I caught a fish; it was in a bucket." She turned her head and winced with pain. "There's the bucket." She pointed to the blue bucket on its side, rolling around in the wind.

"Don't worry about that, we need to get you to a doctor. Can you move?" He placed a firm arm under her back and scooped her up. She gave a short groan and pointed at the bucket again.

"Vicar, it's our supper, I *need* to take it home."

Realising how difficult finances were right now for the Rodriguez family, he understood the urgency in Esperanza's tone. He walked with her in his arms to the bucket, gave it a kick so that it spun around, but he could see it was empty.

Esperanza groaned again. "Someone stole it."

"That maybe so, but we need to get you to the doctor now."

"Please take me home, I just need to rest. I will be fine." She forced a smile in an attempt to convince him.

Albert contemplated her request. She did live nearer than the doctor's office, but she would still need medical attention to her wounds. "Alright, I will take you home and then I will fetch the doctor, you need to get those wounds treated before they become infected."

He carried on up the road with her firmly in his arms. A few minutes later they arrived. Albert, still holding onto Esperanza, despite his back now killing him, kicked against the wooden door.

"It's open," said Esperanza. "It's always open in the day."

Albert tried the handle, still clutching hold of Esperanza and the door, much to his relief, gave way. He rushed inside and placed Esperanza gently down on the sofa. Everything was immaculate, as it always was in the front room, only used to receive guests. She winced as she settled back onto the plump cushions behind her.

"Dorothy!" Albert called out, straightening his back with caution and then went off in search for her. He could hear the excitable shrieks of Jessica and Anna, Esperanza's younger sisters, playing. He followed the noise out to the back garden where he found the two girls, Jessica thirteen years old, tall and lanky and Anna ten years, small and chubby, not alike in appearance, neither did they look like their eldest sister. Anna's jet black neatly braided hair bobbed up and down as she chased Jessica with a strange looking insect. Jessica shrieked with fear while her sister enjoyed every moment of Jessica's torture.

"Girls!" Albert called out sternly, clapping his hands to grab their attention. "Where is your mother?" He asked with a deep frown upon his forehead.

"She's here," Dorothy's voice sounded from behind him. He turned around quickly to face her.

"Oh thank goodness, Dorothy, it's Esperanza."

"What's happened?" Dorothy was suddenly awash with fear, seeing the concerned expression on Albert's face.

"She's had an accident," he said. "I found her in the street not far from the harbour."

Dorothy flung her hand to her mouth and gasped. "How bad? Where is she?"

"In the front room....and..." Before he could say another word, she ran off in search.

Anna dropped the strange looking insect which scurried off into a bush and she followed her mother with Jessica closely in tow.

"I'm going to fetch a doctor," Albert called out after them all and then dashed off through the back garden gate to find help.

"Oh my goodness!" Dorothy examined the wound on her knee.

Anna peered over the sofa. "Wow! That's excellent! It looks like a deep hole." She, drew a hole in the air with her index finger, demonstrating what it looked like. "And there's all gory blood and stuff coming out," she added, grinning.

"You are disgusting, Anna!" Jessica elbowed her in the ribs, and she gave a protesting moan and moved away.

"For goodness sake, girls! Your sister is hurt. Fetch me some clean towels Anna, and Jessica go and get a bowl of warm water." Dorothy leaned over Esperanza, noticing the congealed blood in her hair leading to the back of her head. "Sweetheart, did you hurt your head?" Esperanza nodded gently.

"It's alright, though. Mama please don't fuss." She hated every moment of this attention. Why did she have to fall, she was more annoyed than upset about her injuries.

"I'm your mother and I will fuss all I like." She brushed dark strands of hair from Esperanza's brow.

The girls appeared back in the room. Jessica placed the warm bowl of water on a little side table next to the sofa and Anna placed the clean towels on the floor. Dorothy got to work cleaning her daughter's wounds.

It was an hour and a half later when Albert returned to check up on Esperanza. The doctor had been and gone, unbothered by Esperanza's 'superficial wounds' as he called them, but more concerned that she shouldn't sleep yet due to her bang on the head and a possible concussion. He instructed her to rest but not sleep.

Albert had arrived late for the prayer

service at church and had left five minutes early, explaining he had an important visit to make which was not just to the Rodriguez household but to the fishmongers too. He held out his hand holding a large bream wrapped in brown paper.

"Supper, to replace the one you lost," he announced proudly, handing it to Dorothy. She raised her eyebrows with surprise.

"Lost?" she said, not grasping his meaning.

Esperanza grimaced, she had hoped now that she had lost the fish, she wouldn't need to explain it, but thanks to Albert she would now have to.

"Yes, Esperanza was bringing a fish home for your supper. We think it got stolen. It was not in the bucket." He glanced over at Esperanza.

"Oh no, the bucket!" Esperanza wriggled herself forward, maneuvering her legs to the floor. "I should have taken the bucket. I need to find the bucket. It's not mine."

"Stay there, young lady." Dorothy didn't look impressed.

Albert felt uncomfortable sensing he had just put his foot in it, somehow. "Anyway, I should leave you to it. Enjoy your supper." He made a swift exit.

"Thank you." Dorothy threw an appreciative smile his way as he left the room and then faced her daughter again. Jessica and Anna sat in the two armchairs opposite, intrigued by the story of the missing fish and where it had come from, not to mention their sister's distress over a silly bucket.

Dorothy stood with her hands on her hips. "Esperanza? I'm waiting."

"I went fishing," she replied solemnly.

"With whom? Please don't say the farmer's boy from La Gomera."

Anna sniggered.

"La Gomera?" Jessica echoed.

"Girls take the fish into the other room and go and pick me some tomatoes and a pepper from the yard, if they are ripe enough of course."

They groaned in unison, disappointed at not being able to hear their sister's explanation and left the room.

"I went to return his bucket. He showed me how to fish. I caught a big one." Esperanza's eyes lit up, remembering how big it was and her excitement of catching it.

"Didn't I tell you not to fraternize, and especially with some farmer's boy."

"Why do you keep referring to him in that way."

"Well, that is what he is, isn't it?"

"Yes, but you make it sound shameful. What is wrong with being a farmer?"

Dorothy placed her hands on her hips again. "Nothing. We need farmers, of course we do, but I don't need them hanging around my daughter.

"He's nice. If you met him, you would like him."

Dorothy pursed her lips. "Well, that is not going to happen. I forbid you to go back and see the boy and if I find out that you have disobeyed me, then there will be serious consequences."

A tear trickled down Esperanza's cheek. She couldn't bear the thought of never seeing Carlos again. Even though she did not know him well after only two meetings at the harbour, but she could sense he was as fond of her as she was him.

"But what about his bucket?" she cried.

"What about it? It's lost, which means you don't need to return it. Thank the Lord for small mercies."

"Surely I owe him an explanation?"

"You owe him nothing, least of all an explanation about some old bucket. I will hear no more on the matter. Now rest up. I'm going to prepare supper, a supper donated by the church thanks to you. I'm so embarrassed. Whatever must Albert think of us."

Esperanza pulled her legs up onto the sofa again, leaned back and sobbed into the cushion behind her. She felt like her heart would break and she had no idea why, she was not accustomed to these feelings. Was it love? Whatever it was, it hurt very much, far more than her wounds.

Chapter Eight

"Sweetheart, of course I care about your father. It's just…"

"Just what, Mum?" Alison's voice echoed with annoyance down the phone. "Just that you couldn't give a toss, happy to turn your back on us? Is that it?"

"No! I'm not turning my back on you." Jen sounded equally as annoyed as she sat perched up right on the edge of a sunbed in the garden. "You have your own life; you don't even live at home anymore. Your father and I have not been… well, not great for a long time. There is no reason for us to stay together if we don't make each other happy."

"Those are your words, not Dad's. Mum, he is heartbroken. I've never heard him like that before. He was crying openly on the phone to me, and he said he's even going to turn down the job offer in Bournemouth. He's not thinking straight, you've done this to him."

There was a moment of awkward silence. Jen swallowed the lump at the back of her throat, feeling guilty again. This was so difficult, far more difficult than she envisaged. She never wanted to hurt Alison, or David for that matter. She rested her head back on the sunbed. The afternoon sun felt like a warm hug all over her body, a hug she needed desperately right now. She took a deep breath and then spoke again.

"Alison, your father is just in shock, he just didn't see this coming."

"Oh really?" Alison's sarcasm was heartfelt.

"He will come to terms with it. He hasn't needed me for years, if ever. In fact, most of the time he hardly notices me, he's so busy with work."

"You resent his work, don't you? That's so selfish."

"Of course not. I'm proud of what he has achieved, and I told him not to turn the promotion down. It's just that sometimes, well, nearly all the time, it is lonely living with a man who is married to his job. And for the record I am not selfish. For years I have put you and your father first."

"Did you ever think to speak to him? Tell him how you feel?" Alison asked with a bitter tone, ignoring her mother's comment about putting them first.

"Of course I did, Alison. And he listened at times, but he never really heard."

"What on earth is that supposed to mean?"

"Work it out, you are intelligent enough. Alison, you are a grown woman, you have your life and I have been the best mother I could be to you. I'm sorry you are angry with me. I love you very much and nothing is going to change that."

"Oh yes you love me so much, you never stopped to think how often you will see me, now you are a four-hour flight away, not to mention the cost of getting to you. I'm a student, I don't have money to splash on flights."

"And you don't need to. You know I will pay your ticket. What is the difference if you sit on a train for a few hours to visit me or jump on a plane for four hours?"

"The difference is, I now have to visit my parents in two different places. I can't always come and see you. I'm not going to Tenerife at Easter to see you, if that's what you are thinking." She paced her student dorm up and down in anger. "Dad needs me more than you do, obviously," she added, still seething.

Jen felt like she was losing this battle of a conversation. She took a moment to contemplate what to say next but before she could say anything else in her defence, Alison cut in on her thoughts again.

"I've got to go," she said, annoyed at her mother's silence on the other end of the phone.

"No wait! Alison, I love..."

She was already gone. Jen threw her

mobile phone down onto the sunbed with force. She wanted to scream with frustration. Instead, she grabbed her phone again, stood up and shoved it in the pocket of her denim shorts, ran through into the house and slipped on a pair of pale blue pumps, locked the back door, grabbed her keys, and slammed the front door hard behind her. So hard it sounded like the whole house shook from side to side. She gave it a quick worrisome glance over shoulder and then ran off down the lane.

A few moments later she arrived at the 'Mirador' a viewpoint just a few yards from the little church in La Paz. She plonked herself down on the stone wall, staring down at the dark sandy coastline below. What was she to do? Was Alison right? Was she being selfish thinking she could just up sticks and start a new life without David? Move thousands of miles away from Alison?

"A penny for them?" A female voice from behind with a British accent forced her to turn. But there was no one there. And then she saw the only person remotely close to her, sitting on the wall opposite. A young woman dressed in a black silk dress and wearing a dark chic snug fitting hat. Around her neck she wore a long string of pearls. She looked like she had stepped out of a fancy-dress party set in the 1920's.

"Sorry, were you talking to me?" Jen eyed her cautiously. There was something strange looking about this young woman in her early twenties and it wasn't just her choice of dress. The black seemed to drown her complexion, she was dreadfully pale, she wondered if she might be ill.

"Yes. I didn't mean to intrude. Your thoughts of course are none of my business." Her lips curled into a soft smile. "Although a trouble shared is a trouble halved."

Jen sighed. "If only. I don't think sharing my troubles is going to halve them I'm afraid." She returned the woman's smile and went back to staring out at sea. A moment later she glanced back at the wall and the woman had gone, replaced by a man taking photos of the view and so she turned back to face the view again.

"So, are you going to stay?"

The female voice startled her again and she spun around to see she was not sitting on the wall behind her as she presumed. No one was there.

"How did you...?" asked Jen, perplexed at the swift appearance of the stranger again, this time at her side. The tourist had now left, and it was just the two of them alone once more.

"How did I know that you are trying to decide if you want to stay of leave this beautiful island?"

Jen nodded. "Yes, that, and how did you manage to disappear and then reappear behind me, as if by magic?

"So many questions, this is always the

problem. One should not question everything."

Jen looked down at the young woman's long gloved hands, black to match her dress.

"You are probably right." She sighed looking at her dark, penetrating eyes.

"But if you ask yourself questions, it helps you come to a conclusion, a decision, does it not? Listen to your heart and not your head. The head will rationalise everything too much, give you reasons to do and not to do something, and totally confuse you. The heart will tell you your desire. Your heart's desire outweighs your head, so therefore it must be the one to listen to."

Jen let out a small laugh. "You are absolutely right. My heart's desire is to live here in Tenerife and make a new life for myself. My head argues otherwise."

"Then you must listen to your heart. If you don't you will regret it for the rest of your life."

Jen, feeling emotional again and holding back her tears, focused on the coastline below. "Not easy. I've hurt people, my daughter, my husband."

"They will understand in time. I only wish I had done the same."

"Listen to your heart instead of your head?" Jen asked, still looking out to sea and in particular a couple of fishing boats bobbing up and down against the waves.

"Yes, I should never have listened to my head—regretted it to death."

"Regretted it to death?" Jen repeated her words finding it odd, and then turned to face her, only to find the woman had gone.

Jen jumped to her feet and walked around, searching for any signs of the mysterious woman. But she was nowhere to be seen. How bizarre. Jen frowned and began her walk up the road back to the villa, having calmed down now from her phone call with Alison. And then she spotted the woman again, up ahead.

"Excuse me!" she called out, wishing she had asked her name. "Excuse me! Wait!" Her attempt to gain the woman's attention fell on deaf ears, so Jen quickened her step, but the woman seemed to walk faster. Goodness she was walking up the path of Villa Esperanza! "Sorry, wait! That's my house. Are you looking for me?"

The woman walked around the back of the house and disappeared out of sight. Jen sprinted up the road, down the garden path around the back of the villa, but by the time she had reached the garden, there was no sign of her, only a mysterious trail of pink rose petals that led to the outbuilding, which were definitely not there before when Jen had been sitting in the garden. Jen's attention was suddenly dragged away from the petals to the ring of her mobile phone. She hooked it out of her pocket and answered the call from Kate.

"Hi Jen. I'm sitting in my car waiting for him to leave the house." Kate switched on her windscreen wipers to clear the heavy rain and get a better look at the entrance.

Jen checked her watch, it was already early evening and would be dark over there now, in Tenerife the sun was only just setting, it felt a world away.

"It's pool night, I think. He never misses pool night. He will leave, I'm sure. In fact, I don't think he has ever missed any bank event yet, so even if it isn't pool, it will be something else."

"Dedication for you," Kate smirked.

"Dedication, obsession, whatever it is, who knows what makes that man tick."

"I've got boxes and lots of bags in the boot. So, if you talk me through it, once I get inside, I'll take it all back to mine and pack it properly for the removal people."

"You are an angel. I couldn't have done this without you. I just couldn't face going back and having to deal with him."

"Thank me later. I've got to get in there first, if he ever leaves," Kate said, spotting the front door now opening. "Oh, I think we are on."

David stepped outside and opened a black umbrella against the rain. "Debs, come on or we will be late!" he called out loud from the doorway into the house, so loud that Kate could hear from within her car. She frowned.

"Who's Debs," she whispered loudly, forgetting momentarily that Jen was still on the other end of the line.

"Debs. Oh, some tart who works at the

bank. Strange woman—always gives me the evils whenever she sees me. I have no idea what I have done to upset her, and David always says it's all in my head, very defensive as he always is when it comes to his colleagues."

Debs, dressed in a long pink fur coat, her blonde hair swept up in a bun on top of her head and wearing large heels, appeared at David's side. Her bling, bling, jewellery sparkled from afar. She grabbed his arm and their lips met in a sensual kiss under the umbrella. Kate stared, through the spy hole she had made in the steam on the windscreen, her jaw dropped as she watched on.

"Why do you ask? Kate?" Jen's voice echoed down the line, bringing Kate back to her senses. She picked up the phone again from her lap, not even aware that she had dropped it in her astonishment. "Um, I think it most definitely was not in your head."

"What do you mean? Is she there at the house?" Jen wandered over to a nearby chair in the garden and stat down, all thoughts about the mysterious woman and the trail of rose petals were now long gone.

"Yes, they've just left together, and she got in his car." Kate watched the car drive away.

"Odd. Never had her down as the type to play pool."

"I'm pretty sure they weren't off to play pool by the way she was dressed, and he was pretty spruced up too."

"You mean they were off on a formal event?" She was quickly wracking her brains as to what that could be at this time of the year.

"I don't know, could be a date. They looked quite cozy from where I was sitting." Kate sighed with regret. "Jen, I saw them kiss and I don't mean a peck on the cheek."

There was a stunned silence on the other end of the phone as Jen tried to take in Kate's words. "Are you positive?" she asked finally.

"Yes. I'm so sorry."

"Cheating, lying, bastard and I've been feeling so guilty."

"Well, technically, your marriage is over now, you said you made that clear. But he has moved on rather quickly," Kate grimaced, biting her bottom lip, she hated being the bearer of bad news.

"He has not moved on; he's been with her all this time. It all makes sense now—all those so called 'bank nights' out, his dedication not to miss one—he was seeing her all this time."

"Well, you don't know that for sure," Kate replied tactfully, trying to sooth the situation.

"Oh, I do. That will be why he was quick to say he would not take the job in Bournemouth; he doesn't want to leave her." Everything was falling into place in Jen's mind. "I've been played for a fool, Kate. Trying to make me feel guilty for leaving him, playing on Alison's feelings too, making me look like the bad guy and all the time he..."

"Do you want me to go in now while the coast is clear?" Kate cut in, trying to divert her attention on the practicalities rather than her emotions.

Jen stood up, pushed her shoulders back and said, "no, if we are going to do this, we are going to do it properly." She walked to the front of the property, opened the front door with her key and walked inside the villa. The gecko she had now named Gary, at least she thought it was Gary, they all looked remarkably similar, ran up the wall past the TV. She threw her key down on the coffee table and kicked off her shoes. "While he's at work, I want a man with a van to go and clear the place out."

"What are you going to do with all that furniture? I thought Grace's villa was furnished."

"Oh I don't want it. I will sell it all to the highest bidder, I'm buggered if that bastard is going to keep it."

"Wouldn't he be entitled to half of it?" Kate asked gingerly.

"He'd be entitled to give me a settlement and I know I won't get a penny, being over here and not being able to fight my corner. He'll worm his way out of it, he's as tight as a screw lid on a bottle. This way I will at least get something."

"What about your personal belongings? I can send those onto you."

"Thank you Kate, collect everything with the van, and I will find somewhere to store it all temporarily over there."

"Of course I will, if you arrange it next Thursday, I've got the day off."

"I will arrange everything. I'll put a post on Facebook; it will all sell in no time. Kate, I'm so sorry to drag you into all of this."

"You don't need to apologise. I'm just sorry you had to find out like this. You know I will help in any way that I can. Actually, before you do a post on social media, I've got a friend who has a daughter that has just got married and moving into a new house, she will probably buy quite a lot I would imagine."

"Wonderful! Thank you, you are such a good friend, Kate."

She hung up the phone after saying goodbye. Swept with emotion she was unable to hold back her tears. She sobbed and sobbed until a tap on the door forced her to pull herself together. She wiped her eyes and went to the front door, opened it, only to find no one there. She closed the door and walked back inside then heard a tap, tap, on the glass doors in the kitchen. Petra was waiting, holding a tray of freshly baked cookies. Jen painted on a smile and opened the door.

"Sorry, I probably wasn't quick enough to open the front door."

"Front door? Oh, sorry I didn't think to use the front door, I just find it quicker to nip around the back seeing as we are neighbours." Petra looked concerned, had she overstepped the mark, been too familiar popping in around the back?

"No don't apologise. Sorry, misunderstanding, I thought it was you at the front door just then. It doesn't matter, come in."

"I had an afternoon of baking, as you can see." Petra grinned and then noticed Jen's puffy eyes and sad expression. "Shall I come back, or do you need a friend?"

"I need a friend," Jen cried.

Petra placed the cookies down on the side and then gave her a hug.

"I'm sorry, you must think all I ever do is cry," Jen pulled away from Petra and looked at her with a forlorn expression.

"Of course I don't think that. You are having a difficult time; it's not been easy for you and now you are making life changing decisions."

Chapter Nine

It was almost two weeks since Esperanza's accident and two weeks since she had last seen Carlos. Her mother had done her best to keep her occupied once her leg was healed, all part of a plan to keep Esperanza from meeting that farmer's boy from La Gomera again.

Aware that Carlos would likely be at the harbour as it was Friday, Esperanza managed to finish her mother's tasks around the house and slipped out without her or her sisters knowing. As she approached the harbour her stomach gave a small lurch and she slowed her pace, trying to calm her nerves, unsure if this was the reaction of seeing him again or disobeying her mother, probably both she decided. Carlos had been on her mind every day. The more she tried to forget about him, the more he plagued her mind.

The harbour was busy as usual with

fishing boats coming in and out, each one followed by a flock of shrieking seagulls. She squinted against the sunlight trying to spot his boat. His father always moored it at the far end of the harbour next to the big stone wall at the entrance. There were a few men lined up fishing on the wall to the left of her and a couple to the right, but there was no sign of Carlos. Realising that perhaps he wouldn't be coming today after all, her heart sank. Maybe his father had stopped selling in Puerto De La Cruz or maybe Carlos didn't need to or even want to go with him anymore, after all, she hadn't been at the harbour for the past two weeks. There were so many scenarios running through her mind. She walked away with her head hung low, feeling a strange sense of sadness—similar to loss. What if she never saw him again? That was her mother's wish and it looked like it had been granted. Contemplating whether to risk trying again on the same day next week, or to wait a little longer, she heard her name being called from afar. She gasped, recognizing his voice immediately and turned to see him running towards her. She remained frozen to the spot, trying not to show her nerves too much. A moment later he was standing in front of her, panting, with a bucket and fishing rod in each hand. Her mouth had gone dry, and her palms felt clammy. Now he was in front of her, she wished she had listened to her mother and not come at all.

"Where have you been? I looked out for you

last week and the week before. Don't tell me—you have gone off the idea of fishing?" He beamed, excited to see her.

"I... I..." She became tongue tied and her cheeks deepened in colour.

"What's up?" He could see the worry in her eyes.

"I'm sorry, I...shouldn't be here ...I have to go," she said, finally getting her words out before walking briskly away. What was the point? Her mother had forbidden her to see him and if she found out, she would make life difficult, she had made that very clear. There would be no future in their relationship as much as it pained her to realise this hard fact.

"Why? Have I said something—done something to upset you?" He quickened his step and was now walking by her side matching her pace.

"No, you haven't done anything," she replied marching on.

"Then what is it? I thought we were friends."

"We are, were." She corrected her tense and he picked up on the grammatical change.

"Were?" he echoed, almost running to keep her pace again.

"My mother doesn't like me seeing you."

She hated herself for being so brutally honest, but she couldn't think of anything plausible other than the truth.

"Why not? Your mother has never met me."

"I know, and if she did, I'm sure she would

like you, but..."

"Well, that's easily solved. Do you live far?"

"Yes," she replied and then feeling guilty for lying replied, "no, not really but I don't think it's wise. If she knew that I met you without her permission she...."

"She what? What could she do?" He shrugged his shoulders nonchalantly.

They were now approaching the old fort where ancient cannons still stood the test of time having defended the island from centuries of intruders. There was a small opening in a thick brick wall that created a secret entrance, away from prying eyes. Carlos gently guided her inside.

"We can speak in here, and we won't be seen," he gave a reassuring smile. Cautiously she followed him inside. It was no bigger than a tiny alleyway, fit for only one person at a time. In the olden days they would have used it to run through and up the stairs onto the other side to check for enemies and then back down to set off the cannons, but today it was nothing more than an unused moss-covered passageway. They stood side by side facing the wall in front of them. It would have been impossible to stand at any other angle. He placed his bucket and fishing rod down next to him on the cold, damp floor. She felt his arm brush against hers and a rush of excitement swept over her.

"So, are you going to tell me why your mother doesn't want you to see me?"

Esperanza sighed. "I think it is because

you live on La Gomera, she doesn't know you or your family." She omitted to tell him that more than anything it was because he was a son of a farmer and her mother seemed to dislike that. "She has some silly notion that I should marry a wealthy man one day. It's all nonsense of course and I don't even want to."

"You don't want to get married?" he asked with interest and a hint of disappointment, turning to face her properly.

"I meant get married for wealth. As for getting married, I don't know, maybe one day." She could feel the colour rising in her cheeks again and hoped he wouldn't notice—it was quite dark inside the stone walls.

She shuffled her feet nervously. "Do you want to? Get married I mean..." she asked coyly, finding the courage to look up at him now.

He chuckled. "Yes, I guess, but she must be a wealthy woman. I want to live in a big, fine house and have lots of children. My mother wouldn't settle for anything less."

They both laughed and instinctively he moved towards her. She didn't hesitate, not for a second, and their lips met, locking into a tender kiss. The first kiss either of them had ever had. It was magical, sensational and they were both surprised by the emotions it had stirred deep within, emotions they never knew they had.

"It must have been all that talk about getting married," he joked, stroking the side of her face.

She giggled and kissed his cheek.

"I think this should be our new meeting place," he said, but his smile quickly faded to a look for concern. "You are going to see me again?"

She nodded her head. "Yes, I will."

"What about your mother?" Carlos watched her closely. She seemed to be almost scared of her mother. The worry was back in her eyes again.

"I'll find a way," she said, sounding more confident than she looked. "After a kiss like that, how could I resist? She added, managing a small smile.

"Well, I suppose, I mean I am irresistible," he grinned.

She playfully punched his arm and he pretended to be wounded, making her laugh even more.

After sealing their newfound love with another kiss, she left the old fort before him and he was careful to wait five minutes before leaving too.

On a high, Esperanza walked home. She felt like she was walking on air, a feeling in her heart of utter and complete happiness and she hoped the feeling would last forever.

Chapter Ten

"What the hell have you done?" David shouted down the phone. "I've been completely robbed—cleared out and I know it was you because there was no forced entry and John across the road told me a man with a van turned up, then your 'stuck up' friend, Kate, pulled up moments later."

"Quite the detective. And she is not stuck up!" Jen sipped on a gin and tonic, then relaxed back on her sun lounger, enjoying every moment of her revenge.

"Well? What have you done with it all? You didn't even leave me a bed to sleep in."

"Oh, I'm sure Debs can provide you with a bed, seeing as you have been sharing ours since I've been gone."

So she knew, that was what all this was about. David ran his fingers nervously through his hair. This was her retaliation. He paced up and down the living room floor like a caged tiger.

"It's not what you think it is," he said, standing before the curtainless window, watching a robin hop around the front garden searching for worms after a recent downpour.

"Oh please, give me some credit. David, you might have pulled the wool over my eyes before, leading me to believe you had a hectic social life with the bank etc...."

"I did... I do..." he intercepted, jumping to his defense.

"You were with *her*," she hissed the words and sat up straight, almost spilling her G&T. "In answer to your question, I've sold the bloody lot."

"No! No, you can't do that!" He was back to pacing the room again, holding the phone so tightly his knuckles were turning white. "My record collection, my personal belongings, family photographs or my parents, my banking certificates, pool medals."

"Relax, all personal things are in the loft, I'm not that cruel, but everything else is sold. And you are dam lucky that I'm so easy going or I would have sold everything including your precious belongings!" She hung up, having had enough of his moaning. A second later a text message came in from him.

"You're not getting anything else, not a penny for this house or our savings, I'm freezing our joint account. YOU WILL GET NOTHING!!!"

"Tell me something I don't know," she

mumbled walking across the garden and back into the kitchen to top up her drink.

Adding a new lump of ice, she watched it sizzle as it hit the tonic, and wiped her tears with a tissue that she dug out of her pocket. She knew her marriage had ended years ago, but there was no going back now after what he had done. Not ever. She thought clearing out the house would have helped her feel better, only it didn't, it just made her miserable to think that they had ended twenty-three years of marriage so bitterly.

A tap on the front door grabbed her attention. She placed her glass down on the kitchen side, wondering if it was one of those mysterious knocks on the front door again— the ones where she opened it only to find no one there. Prepared, she flung open the door

"Alison! Oh my God!"

Alison stood on the doorstep with a small blue suitcase and a rucksack hanging from her shoulder. She looked every image of her mother, from the auburn long hair scraped up in a high ponytail to the smattering of freckles on her nose.

Jen hugged her tightly but soon noticed her hug was not being returned. Alison stood rigidly, seemingly annoyed at her mother.

"I'm not here on some pleasure trip," she said at last. "I'm here to speak some sense into you!"

She brushed past her mother, wheeling her suitcase into the living room, and then dumping her rucksack onto the sofa.

Jen followed her into the room. "How did you know the address here? And how to find your way?" she added looking puzzled.

"Mother, I'm twenty-one years old, I think I'm capable of finding my way to Tenerife, even if it is some remote island across the waters from the Sahara Desert! If you must know, I got your address off Kate."

"Kate? Why on earth didn't she tell me?" Jen stood with her hands on her hips baffled by Alison's surprise arrival, not to mention the frosty reception she was receiving from her.

"Because I told her it was a surprise. She's so gullible." Alison flopped down on the sofa and kicked off her trainers.

Jen screwed up her nose at the disgusting odour. "Please be more respectful, Kate is a good friend."

"Oh yes, she burgled Dad—with friends like that who needs enemies? He called me, told me all about your antics."

"I bet he did. Drink?" Jen asked, walking away, in the direction of the kitchen, trying to keep calm.

"Got anything cold? A beer?"

"As it happens, yes I do." A moment later Jen appeared back in the living room with a glass of beer in her hand. The stench of Alison's sweaty feet hit her again and she stopped in her tracks to regain her breath.

"After this, please take a shower, your feet stink!"

"Yes, well it's bloody hot here and I've been

110

travelling since the early hours of the morning—what do you expect?" She grabbed the beer from her mother and took a large swig, enjoying the coolness as it the hit the back of her throat. She then stopped and burped, wiping the foam from her top lip with the back of her hand.

"How long are you staying for, darling?" Jen smiled, in an attempt to sooth the situation and ignore her daughter's bad manners for now, not feeling up to another row.

"Four days, hopefully enough time to make you realise you are making the biggest mistake of your life."

Jen laughed out loud. "I think you are being a tad melodramatic."

"Really? So, leaving Dad, your home, your job—even me, to live in your dead friend's house, thousands of miles away, practically in Africa, is perfectly acceptable?"

"Alison, there's things you don't know, about your father."

"Oh really. Go on then, I'm all ears." She took another swig of beer, her angry eyes still fixed on her mother.

It had been threatening to rain but fortunately the sun had made an appearance and the grey clouds were starting to disappear. It meant that the church fete didn't need to be held inside after all. Albert was thrilled at the sight of so many stalls. There was everything from clothes, children's toys, handmade crafts, to paintings and much more. Dorothy and Mary each had a stall next to each other selling homemade cakes. Esperanza was involved in handing them out and accepting payment while her two sisters played with the other children in the church gardens.

"I think we've done a great job; these cakes are going down a treat," Mary said with pride.

"Aren't they just, particularly the Victoria Sandwich cakes," Dorothy pointed to a row of them neatly displayed on plates on top of a white linen clothed table. "I'd better go and check on the other stalls, after all, Vicar has trusted me to make sure it all runs smoothly," she said proudly, clearly happy to be of use.

Mary smiled, knowing full well this was a purpose made job created by Vicar Albert Jones and herself to help Dorothy earn some money, but so far Dorothy hadn't cottoned on. It wouldn't be much, although enough to help tide her over with food money for a little while.

"Espe, watch the stall," she instructed her daughter, before walking off with her head held high, shoulders pushed back and looking every inch the person in charge.

Esperanza stood up and moved to the

middle of the table. An annoying fly was hovering over one of the cakes and she shushed it away with her hand. Then a wasp followed much to her dismay. Mary was busy serving customers so Esperanza couldn't ask her for help. Instead, she grabbed a gardening magazine from the table behind that her mother had brought with them, in case there should be any quiet moments, and swooped it at the wasp almost knocking the cake on the floor. She grabbed the cake, steadying it but the angry wasp was out for revenge buzzing around her ear. She let out a huge scream and ran around the other side of the table tripping straight into the arms of a passing gentlemen.

"Sorry, so sorry," she said, embarrassed and trying to compose herself while checking around to see if the wasp was still following her.

"I hate wasps too," he said in English but with a broad Spanish accent. She looked up at him. He was a tall man in his early to mid-twenties wearing an expensive suit and holding a leather briefcase. He had witnessed the whole commotion from the start and displayed an expression of amusement. Esperanza, red faced, nodded, and walked around the other side of the table again.

"I like the look of that Upside-Down Pineapple cake, but then again I love Victoria Sandwich too." He dragged his eyes back to meet Esperanza's. "Which one would you recommend?"

"Um, well…" She seemed still ruffled by the incident of the wasp and somewhat amazed that he spoke such good English, natives to the island rarely did.

"Both are nice," she replied at last.

"Well then I will take both," he grinned.

"Oh. Wonderful. I will put them in a box for you."

"Are you from Tenerife?" he asked, picking up on her twang. If she was, she spoke excellent English he mused.

"No. Half Spanish, half English," she answered matter of fact, while placing the cakes each into their own small cardboard boxes.

"That explains your impeccable English." He pulled out his wallet and placed a few large notes, far more than the cakes were worth, into the payment pot on the table.

This didn't go unnoticed to Esperanza. "Oh, the cakes are not that much."

"I'm sure they will be worth every peseta," he smiled."

"Well, that is most kind." This time she returned his smile.

"What was most kind?" Dorothy asked, appearing at Esperanza's side having satisfied her rounds of the stalls. Mary was still busy chatting to customers, her cakes were almost sold out.

"This gentleman gave a generous payment for the Upside-Down Pineapple cake and the Victoria Sandwich," Esperanza explained.

The gentleman removed his hat

courteously. "I'm sure they will be more than worth the money. I shall share them with my parents, my father in particular will never say no to cake."

Dorothy was impressed. "What incredible English you have," she remarked.

"I studied in England for two years. My father insisted it would be good for business."

"And what business may that be?" He had definitely gained Dorothy's interest.

"The jewellery business," he answered, proudly.

Suddenly realisation dawned on Dorothy. "Are you the son of the owner of Joyeria De Sanchez by any chance?"

"Yes, I am," he smiled. "Do you know my father?"

"We only met the once many years ago at a party in Santa Cruz. My late husband introduced him to me, he seemed a pleasant man, so I recall. You are the image of him." She leaned closer and said in a quiet voice, as if not wishing to divulge a top secret, "I heard you have opened a larger shop in Santa Cruz and looking to open another here in Puerto De La Cruz - is this true?"

Esperanza watched from the sidelines with both interest and embarrassment for her mother's outlandish behaviour.

He moved in closer too, surreptitiously mocking her behaviour. "Yes, it is," he said in a hushed voice. "I'm here on a mission of research. To see if there would be a strong enough clientele for the area."

"So, you thought foreign market, try the British church." She raised her eyebrows. "I like you're thinking," she added with a small smile.

"Yes, correct." He laughed, taking a step back.

"And your conclusion is?" she asked.

"I'm not entirely sure yet, but it's possible."

"Well, I hope so. This place needs an upmarket jewellery shop and I for one would welcome it.

Esperanza stared at her mother in disbelief, she couldn't afford to put food on the table let alone buy jewellery. Yet she still liked to give the impression she had money.

"Where are my manners? Dorothy Rodriguez and this is my daughter Esperanza," she quickly pointed out, eager for the two of them to be acquainted properly.

"Alfredo Sanchez," he kissed Dorothy's hand and then Esperanza's. Esperanza quickly pulled away and wiped her hand on the back of her dress. If there was one thing she detested, it was smarmy men. He picked up the boxes of cakes, thanked them both and went on his way.

"What a fine young man," Dorothy swooned as her eyes followed him. "If only I was twenty years younger!"

"Did I miss something?" Mary asked, now her customers had all gone.

"Yes, you did Mary. We both had the great pleasure of meeting Alfredo Sanchez. You know Joyeria de Sanchez, jewellers?"

"Oh really?" Mary hadn't a clue what Dorothy was talking about but knew better than to show lack of interest.

"What a splendid young man and not a farmer's boy either." Dorothy gave a sly sideways glance at her daughter.

Mary was still lost by it all. "Not a farmer's boy?"

Esperanza rolled her eyes and sighed heavily. Her mother didn't even know she had been secretly meeting Carlos these past few weeks, yet she still hadn't forgotten. "Mother doesn't like farmers apparently," Esperanza explained indignantly.

"That's not true Esperanza and you know it. I just have high hopes for you. Anyway, I'm glad that silly nonsense is all in the past now."

***

Alison placed her mobile phone down on the coffee table after speaking to her father and looked over at her mother remorsefully.

"I'm so sorry, Mum. I can't believe he did that to you."

Jen sat down on the sofa opposite and tucked her feet under her bottom, the way she always liked to sit. "So, he admitted it to you then?"

Alison wiped away her tears with one of the fluffy cushions she was hugging. The news of her father cheating on her mother had come as a shock, especially as he had not denied it

117

when she called him.

"More than admitted it, he had the cheek to tell me it wasn't an affair, he..." She suddenly stopped mid flow, realising she should spare her mother any further pain.

"Go on."

"He wants me to meet her, well, he can go and take a running jump, no way will I meet her!" Alison ranted.

"Are you hungry?" Jen asked, changing the subject.

Alison stared back at her mother, puzzled by her random question and her apparent lack of care about it all. "Um well yes, I'm always hungry."

Jen smiled wryly. "Come on. I'm going to take you to a lovely local restaurant around the corner and on the way, I have something I want to show you."

Alison seemed to perk up. "OK, now I'm intrigued. Does that mean I can have a shower and wash my stinky feet when I get back? I'll just go and squirt some deodorant on them and run a brush through my mop."

"Go on then, I guess they won't smell through your trainers," Jen replied. "I'll show you where the bathroom is. Gary might be in there though."

"Gary?" Good God, did her mother have a boyfriend already? Jen was quick to pick up on her worried expression.

"Gary is the resident gecko. Don't worry, he's friendly and for some reason he likes to hang out in the bathroom—takes ages in there."

"Oh, typical male then," Alison gave a hoot, relieved that Gary wasn't human. "Oh, by the way, where am I sleeping? Please not in Grace's room that would be just too creepy."

Jen scratched her head in thought, she had not considered about what would happen if Alison came to stay, it had happened so unexpectedly. She didn't feel comfortable sleeping in Grace's room either.

"There's two beds in my room, if you don't mind bunking up with your old mum."

"OK, I think I can live with that, just for a few nights."

"As long as you have washed your feet, mind," Jen chided.

"Of Course!" Alison flashed her best beguiling smile.

Jen, delighted to have Alison with her and pleased that she no longer resented her for leaving her father, felt happy to have her back. They linked arms as they walked away from the house, chatting animatedly. They were too busy to have noticed the ghostly face, watching them from the bedroom window.

"This is what I wanted to show you." Jen pulled Alison towards the 'Mirador' viewpoint, excitedly.

"Wow!" Alison placed the palms of her hands on the stone wall and bent over to get a better look. "Is that Puerto De La Cruz town?"

"Yes. Beautiful, isn't it?"

"Yes, it really is but why is the sand black?"

"The island is volcanic; it naturally has black sand."

Alison sat down on the wall. "So, are all the beaches black on the island? It's so weird to see black sand. I'm not sure if I like it or love it."

Jen sat down too. "Not all beaches on Tenerife are black. Playa Teresitas beach in Santa Cruz has white sand and lots of beaches in the south do too. They imported the sand from the Sahara for those beaches."

"So why didn't they do the same for this beach?" She pointed to the stretch of black coastline below them again.

Jen shrugged. "Maybe the locals like it, find it more authentic, personally I think it should remain black."

"And what is that water fountain and big pool thing over there?"

"That's the Lago Martiánez, it's an open-air swimming pool complex, it's really beautiful. Maybe we could go tomorrow?"

"Yes, I would love that," Alison replied, eyes gleaming like a small child. She reminded Jen of when she was a little girl, when she got excited to go to the park or on a picnic— she loved going on picnics in the summer.

"I come here a lot," Jen admitted. "With all the trouble with your Dad, it helped to clear my head." Jen frowned. "I met an eccentric young lady here and we chatted, she was dressed like she was going to a 1920's fancy dress party."

Alison turned to face her mother. "Eccentric in what way?"

"Like I said, her clothes, they were old fashioned—loves to wear black—her face was so pale."

Alison gave a short hoot of laughter. "She's a Goth, Mum, that's what they call them, not *an eccentric young lady*."

"I don't think she is, unless Goths dress up in 1920's costumes, do they?"

"Yes, sure they do, they like anything vintage. Have you never seen a Goth before?"

"I'm not really sure what constitutes a Goth, I mean maybe not all pale looking people wearing black clothes are Goths."

"Well, if you want to see Goths, there's plenty in Whitby, it's a fishing town up north in Yorkshire."

"Yes, I do know where Whitby is, thank you Alison," Jen chided playfully. "Don't forget I am an English literature teacher and have read Bram Stoker's Dracula with the kids in class many times."

"Oh yes, Whitby is Dracula land alright, hence the reason for all the Goths hanging out there. So surely you must know what a Goth looks like from the books?"

"Never paid much attention to Goths in books, but from what I remember, they seemed to be heavily made up with makeup and this lady wasn't. Anyway, enough about Goths, Dracula, and Whitby, let's get some food, I'm hungry." She didn't want to tell Alison about how the same lady had entered Villa Esperanza grounds and left a trail of rose petals leading to the outbuilding—it all seemed so far-fetched that Alison would surely doubt her mother's sanity. She, herself found it to be insane and put it down to her mind playing tricks or anxiety due to the stress of everything she had been through lately, losing Grace and then the upset with David, the mind can do strange things when one is stressed.

The restaurant was busy inside and quiet outside, as usual. There was a noticeable chill in the air this evening, but the terrace fires were burning and so the two women decided to sit outside where it was less rowdy. No sooner had they sat down, the waiter was straight out to greet them and handed them the menu. He recognised Jen immediately, smiling from ear to ear.

"I see you have a friend with you this evening." He handed Alison a menu.

"This is my daughter, Alison," Jen corrected him, proudly.

"Very nice to meet you. Ladies we have some specials this evening..." He rattled off several dishes and did his very best to translate them into English. A few minutes later, after taking their orders of various tapas, he was gone.

"Well, this is nice, I didn't think I would be having dinner with my daughter this evening, when I woke up this morning." She reached out and touched Alison's hand. "It's so good to see you."

"It's good to see you too, Mum." Alison sat back in her chair, relaxed, brushing all thoughts of her father away. What was important now was making sure her mother knew what she wanted to do with her life. And it was time to find out. "I can see why you like it here. Is the plan to stay here forever?" she asked, searching her mother's face for an honest answer.

"Forever is a long time, but I can't see me going back to England, well not any time soon."

"I get it, I really do. First, Grace dies, leaves you a beautiful house and money; setting you up nicely here and then Dad does the dirty on you. I think I would stay too if I were in your shoes."

"Really?" Jen frowned, trying to determine if Alison really meant it.

"Yes, I think I would," she confirmed.

The waiter served them wine and left the bottle on the table.

"Cheers!" Jen held up her glass and Alison did the same.

"To a new future," Alison toasted as the glasses clinked together. "So, if you stay here, what are you going to do? I mean you are not that old that you need to retire yet."

"Thanks, I'll take that as a compliment!" Jen took another sip of her wine.

"It was meant to be a compliment. You've still got so much to give. I'm guessing you have left your job at the school?"

"Yes, I did. I feel terrible about my abrupt departure, but they've been brilliant—so understanding, more than I deserve leaving them in the lurch like that." Jen sighed wistfully. "I used to love teaching, but like anything, if you do it for too long you get burnt out. I felt that I was acting on autopilot most of the time when I was in the classroom. The passion of teaching disappeared a long time ago.

"Maybe it will come back after taking a break," Alison said thoughtfully.

"Or maybe I just need a complete change," Jen replied honestly. "There's an outbuilding to the villa. I've been thinking of doing something with it. Grace wanted to but never got around to it."

"Do what exactly?" Alison's eyes lit up "Teach yoga?"

Jen nearly choked on her wine. "Me? Teach yoga? I know nothing about yoga, never taken a lesson in my life."

"You can learn and then become a teacher," Alison suggested encouragingly. "It's all the rage—yoga lessons."

"No, I don't think yoga is really for me. I was thinking more along the lines of making it into a self-contained holiday apartment and get a rental income.

"Great idea! Maybe offer B&B too, you are a great cook when you make the effort,"

Alison grinned.

"Thanks, I'll take that as another compliment." Jen chuckled. "I do enjoy cooking when I have the time, but that has not been possible for quite some time."

"Well now you have the time. Hey, you could even offer cooking holidays, have a bit of a theme going on." Alison was getting carried away again. "You know, cake baking weeks—dinner party weekends."

Jen laughed. "Me a cookery teacher?"

"Yeah, why not?"

The waiter placed a bowl of tomato soup in front of Alison and prawns in a hot garlic oil in front of Jen, known by the locals as Gambas Al Pil-Pil.

"Mmm looks delicious," Jen put her nose in the air to inhale the aroma.

Alison looked inquisitively at the sizzling prawns. "See, you could be banging out dishes like that."

Jen grinned. "Yeah, maybe I could, who knows." Alison had a way of building up her confidence, helping her to think she could achieve anything and that she was never too old to learn. She needed to hear that more than ever and was grateful for her encouragement.

"Great, that's you sorted then. Oh, and I want to be involved in the interior décor," Alison said matter of fact.

"Of course!" Jen looked thrilled. "Hey, a girls' day out in Santa Cruz shopping for soft furnishings, what could be better?"

"Absolutely!" Alison agreed, tucking into her soup.

The two women chatted throughout the rest of their meal, they were more like old friends than mother and daughter. By the time they ordered their desserts, the inside of the restaurant had become quieter, until a group of rowdy men arrived, chatting, laughing, and joking. Amongst them was Carlos Garcia. Noticing Jen straight away, he left his friends and made a beeline for their table.

"Jen! How wonderful to see you again! And I see you have your sister with you tonight." He flashed that charming smile of his at both women. Jen, feeling the colour rise in her cheeks, laughed. He was joking right? He couldn't possibly think that Alison was her sister.

"Charming as ever," she replied, now fully aware that she was definitely blushing. "This is Alison, my daughter."

"Hi," Alison greeted him with intrigue, especially noticing the effect he seemed to be having on her mother.

"Daughter? My goodness." He looked genuinely surprised. "Well, I can certainly see the likeness. What is that wonderful English saying?" He scratched his head in a playful thought.

"Apple doesn't fall far from the tree?" Alison said in earnest.

"Nope, it's not that, something to do with

peas."

"Two peas in a pod?" Jen and Alison blurted out in unison.

"My point exactly!" He laughed. "Can I buy you two lovely ladies a drink?"

"Yes, I'll have a vodka and tonic please." Alison was a bit too quick to answer, which made them laugh again.

"Jen?" he asked, turning his attention fully to her, holding her stare.

"Oh, a Rioja please," she replied, trying to keep cool.

She looked more relaxed than last time he had seen her, which jogged his memory about something. "I saw you the other day sitting at the Mirador."

Jen appeared surprised. "Oh, I didn't see you. You should have said hello."

"I would have but you were talking on the phone, well, I think you were. Either that or you talk to yourself because no one was there," he laughed.

"Gosh, I'm getting senile, I honestly don't remember speaking on the phone when I was at the Mirador or speaking to myself." She blushed again.

"Nonsense! Nothing senile about you. Let me get you those drinks."

The moment he left the table, Alison leaned forward. "Man, is he into you or what!"

"Alison!"

"And I'd say the feeling is pretty mutual by the colour of your face."

"Stop it! He's married."

"Really? That's such a bummer. Are you sure he's married?"

"Well he has a son, and he says 'we' when speaking about his family life, so I'm guessing so."

"Only one way to find out, ask him."

Jen was horrified. "Don't you dare! That would be so embarrassing and anyway, it doesn't matter if he is, or not. I'm married to your father may I remind you."

"May I also remind you that my father is a cheating, lying, scumbag and you deserve better."

"Alison, have some respect. Whatever he's done, he is still your father, and you cannot speak about him like that."

Alison sunk back in her seat, like a naughty schoolgirl that had just been chastised.

Jen fell quiet too. Had she really been speaking to herself when Carlos saw her? She was not aware that she did that. How embarrassing.

Overthinking again? Don't doubt yourself, he's fond of you.

The question, followed by advice sounded gentle, kind although intrusive to her train of thought. She instinctively looked over at Alison. "Did you say something?"

"No," Alison shook her head, taking a swig of wine.

Surprised to realise the voice must have

come from inside of her own head, Jen took a large gulp of wine.

Chapter Eleven

The clock overpowered the silence in the dinning room. Jessica and Anna inspected the tiny bit of meat on their plates next to the small handful of green beans and one lonely, boiled potato, which made the plate look so much bigger than it actually was. Esperanza was also unimpressed at the tiny portion of food sitting before her.

Dorothy sighed heavily, looking at all three of their grim faces. "You shouldn't eat too much before bed, it's bad for the digestion." They all knew the reason for the small amount of food was nothing to do with their mother's care for their digestion, it was purely due to their lack of money. Dorothy forced a cheerful smile. "I've decided to sell the house," she announced, taking them all by surprise.

"Where would we live, Mama?" Jessica asked with a deep frown creasing her young forehead. She always looked like she carried the weight of the world on her small thirteen-year-old shoulders.

"Well, I've been speaking to Auntie Mary in Hampshire, she will let us stay there until we find a nice little home in the countryside."

Esperanza looked horrified. "Hampshire, in England?"

"Yes Espe, Hampshire in England."

"Yes!" Anna's eyes danced with excitement. "I read a book about insects in England, and they have many spiders—indoor ones too—really big ones."

"Well, that's it, I'm definitely not going," Jessica pouted and with fear growing in her eyes, not just at the thought of the spiders, which Anna was clearly reveling in, but the idea of leaving Tenerife, leaving her home and her friends."

"Anna! What is your obsession with creepy crawlies? Honestly, you should have been born a boy," Dorothy scolded. "Jessica, there are no more spiders in England than there are here. Well maybe just a few more, but they are harmless."

Esperanza sat quietly with tears rolling down her cheeks, full of dismay. How could her mother do this? Take her away from Carlos, her home, the place she had grown up, where they had lived practically all their lives?

"Don't look so glum Jessica and Espe, we need money, and the best thing for me to do is sell the house."

"Why don't you just buy a smaller and cheaper one here?" Esperanza said, wiping the stinging tears from her eyes with her fingers. Surely that was the logical explanation to the problem?

"Because, sooner or later, the money will run out again. In England, I am more employable, and we will have support, we have family there."

"Family we've never met," Jessica grumbled.

"Well you soon will," Dorothy retorted. This was not going as well as she had hoped. Only Anna seemed happy at the prospect of moving to England.

"We will get a lovely home and I'll even get you a dog or a cat, or both if you like," she said, trying to win them over.

"I don't want a dog or a cat." Esperanza stood up and ran out of the room.

"Me neither!" Jessica ran after her sister.

"Girls!" Dorothy raised her voice. "You haven't asked permission to leave the table." Her voice fell on deaf ears, they had already left the room.

Anna eyed her sisters' plates either side of her. "If they don't want their supper, can I have it, Mama?"

Dorothy nodded reluctantly. "Yes, I suppose."

"And I'd love a dog and a cat," Anna added.

The sky was overcast the following morning when Dorothy made her way up the little lane towards the bakery with just enough money for a loaf of bread that would have to last them at least five days, according to her budget she'd worked out.

Mary was coming out of the bakery as Dorothy entered and they collided.

"Oh Dorothy, I'm so sorry!" She looked elegant as usual in a cornflower blue dress and her hair swept neatly behind her head. "How did they take the news?" She asked eagerly.

Dorothy gave a her a blank look. "News?" she was preoccupied with thinking about what she could cook with the little ingredients left in the pantry.

"The girls, about moving to England," Mary prompted.

"Oh, well Jessica and Esperanza are not happy to say the least, but Anna is thrilled to go because of the spiders."

Mary looked confused.

Dorothy shook her head. "Don't ask!"

"I see," Mary said. "Is there any other way? I will miss you terribly."

Dorothy shrugged her shoulders. "I wish there were. To be honest I don't really want to go. It is rather gloomy in England, with all that rain and endless grey skies, but unless I find a rich man and quick, I don't have a choice," she said wryly. Mary realised that she was in fact joking, about finding a rich man, she gave her a sympathetic pat on the arm and then said goodbye, feeling rather deflated that she couldn't help Dorothy's situation.

When Dorothy left the bakery with a loaf of bread that smelt so good, she could have eaten it there and then, she thought about her conversation with Mary. Of course she wouldn't find a man on this island, not a wealthy one or even a poor one for that matter. There had only ever been one man for Dorothy, and he was gone forever. The thought of meeting someone new was quite preposterous. But she suddenly had an idea. Esperanza will soon be eighteen. She was young, pretty and if she were to marry a wealthy man, she would be in the position to help her own family and save them from leaving the island. She smiled with excitement. That was it! She knew just the man—Alfredo Sanchez! She couldn't think of a more perfect match. Or a more perfect solution to their financial situation. Why on earth hadn't she thought about it earlier?

With her knees tucked up under her chin, Esperanza sat as close as she could to Carlos, behind the big black cannon at the old fort, sheltering from the wind. Her eyes were sore from crying.

"If I could offer you a home, a future, I'd ask you to marry me right here and now," Carlos said, feeling hopeless. "But you deserve more than to live in a house no better than a shack on a farm, on some remote island that the rest of the world have never heard of—apart from you," he added and smiled softly.

"Now you sound like my mother," she said, turning to face him, looking forlorn. "I would live in a hole if it meant being with you for the rest of my life."

"Espe, you don't belong in a hole no more than you belong on a rambling old farm. And your mother is right."

"So what are you saying?" There was a slight tremor to her voice. *Did he not love her anymore?*

He took a deep breath and then reached out for her hand, taking it into his own. He squeezed it gently. "I'm saying, I love you. I love you so much that it hurts—it hurts to let you go, but you must go back to England and find a better future, not just for you but for your family too."

She knew he was right, but the truth hurt. Anger flowed over her, lashing out at him because she hated the situation she found herself in, she cried "No! You are not going to use this as an excuse to end what we have. If you don't want to be with me—marry me—then fine—but don't send me packing to England to clear your conscience."

She stood up, tears streaming down her face. "Goodbye Carlos," she sobbed and then walked briskly away from him. He immediately jumped to his feet and ran after her.

"Wait! Espe!" Arriving at her side, he pulled her arm in attempt to stop her from walking.

"Leave me alone! You've made it very clear

you don't want me."

"That's not true. If things were different, if I could..."

"If, if, if," she shouted at him and then ran off leaving him speechless.

This time he decided not to run after her. It was no good, there was no reasoning with her, and his heart was breaking too. Instead, he walked around the corner and out of sight. With anger brewing about the situation, they were now faced with, in a small, narrow alleyway he punched the wall, causing his knuckles to bleed. The pain was nothing compared to the heartache he was feeling as he dropped to the floor and sobbed, knowing he would probably never see her again. But still, deep inside, he knew he had to let her go. It was the right thing to do.

Jen and Alison sat at the breakfast table in the kitchen this morning instead of outside, owing to the heavy rain and thunderstorms.

"This storm better move on by tomorrow afternoon. I don't want to be taking off in bad weather," Alison said, sipping a hot cup of tea. She didn't mind flying but was not brave when there was turbulence.

"Don't worry, it will all be over by tonight, I

checked the weather forecast," Jen reassured her. "I'm going to miss you," she added, dreading saying goodbye. It never got any easier and especially now that she was not in the same country. A part of her still felt guilty for creating that distance between them, but she knew in her heart she would rather be waiting to see her in Tenerife than in England. "Oh my God!" She suddenly placed her coffee mug down with force, oblivious to it spilling all over the table.

"What?" Alison, confused, watched her mother rush to the patio doors and pull them open.

"Hey! Are you looking for me?" She shouted out above the sound of the wind whistling and the rain that was now lashing heavily. The woman in black was standing at the door of the outbuilding on the other side of the garden. She seemed not to care or even notice the wind and rain battering her dress and her hair that was now loose and whipping against her pale face.

Jen, quickly doing up her dressing gown, ran outside. Her slippers squelched through the sodden lawn.

"Lady, I'm here! Over here!" She shouted again, then stopped momentarily to brush her wet hair from her eyes. Then she saw the door was open to the outbuilding and the woman had gone inside. Panting, she too followed, but there was no one there. "Hello?" The cold open space sent shivers down her spine. The rain pelted against the large window behind her, and the door slammed shut from the wind as she spun around to face it. "Hello?" Her trembling voice sounded flat in the deathly stillness of the room. This was all too creepy. Where had she gone? She stood in the middle of the room and glanced around. Nothing. No trace of the woman.

"Mum!" Alison flung open the door, her blue, silk, pyjamas clinging to her body, barefoot, water pouring downwards, creating a big puddle on the stone floor beneath her. "What the hell is going on?" She demanded to know, forcing Jen's attention back to reality.

"Oh my goodness you are soaked. We need to get you dried up." Jen looked at her, horrified.

"And so are you!" Jen glanced down at her dressing gown and slippers.

"Yes, true. Come on let's go back indoors."

When they were both dry and dressed Jen made a hot drink and they sat down again at the kitchen table. She stared vacantly at the rain on the glass door. It didn't make sense, the woman opened the door, went in, then disappeared. How did she get out—there was no other exit?

"So, are you going to tell me why you ran out like a possessed woman in the pouring rain in your dressing gown?" Alison stared at her mother, waiting for her explanation.

Jen dragged her attention back to Alison's question. "The woman in black—the eccentric one—she was there, she went into the outbuilding."

"I didn't see anyone, are you sure?"

"Yes, I'm certain. It was the same woman I saw at the Mirador."

"The goth?"

"You call her a goth, I don't."

Alison shook her head in despair. "Anyway, why would she be in the outbuilding? How did she even get in there, surely, it's locked? And how come she wasn't there when I turned up?" This was all sounding a bit farfetched, and she was beginning to wonder if her mother was losing the plot.

"No, the door is never locked, I can't find the key. I don't know why she was there, I just saw her approach, then the door opened, and she went inside. And then I went in after her and she was gone."

"Mum, I think maybe you are seeing things, the stress is getting to you, what with Grace passing, then you splitting up with Dad, it can play havoc on the mind, maybe even make you think you've seen things that are not there."

"That's what I thought when it happened before, but not this time." Jen knew this time what she saw was real.

"Wait! This has happened before?"

Alison looked worried.

"Yes, I wasn't going to tell you but after I saw her at the Mirador, she appeared up ahead of me on my way back home. And when I got to the garden, all I found was a trail of rose petals." She got up and walked towards the cupboard, opened it and pulled out a pack of chocolate biscuits. "Do you want one?" She opened the packet and held it out for Alison to take one. Alison shook her head, bemused at her mother's nonchalant behaviour.

"I'm worried about you, Mum, worried about leaving you tomorrow and you being here alone. I think you need to see a doctor."

"Oh nonsense, I'm fine." Jen gave a dismissive wave. "Besides, Petra will be back soon from visiting her friend in Germany, I'm not alone." She dunked a biscuit into her coffee and took a bite. When she had cleared her mouth she said, "shame you didn't get to meet her—Petra that is—not the eccentric woman obviously," she laughed sardonically.

Alison studied her mother. It was hard to tell who the parent was these days. She seemed different, more carefree but her behaviour was certainly worrying. She only hoped it was down to the recent big changes in her life and nothing more serious.

"You can meet her next time you are back," Jen concluded.

"Yes, I'm sure I will. Are you going to put a swimming pool in?" Alison asked, changing the subject, there was no point continuing the conversation about some goth woman who had supposedly turned up and then disappeared.

Jen nodded. "Yes, I think it will be more inviting for people to come and stay if I do, don't you think?"

"Absolutely! You won't get me out of it when I come to stay."

The rain had now subsided, and the sun was poking through the breaking grey clouds.

"Looks like it's stopping." Jen observed the garden, having opened the patio doors. "We should do something, it's your last day. What do you fancy doing?"

"Anything, I don't mind," Alison looked down at her bare feet. "I'll go and put my shoes on."

Jen stepped outside. The humidity was rising and a strong scent from the soaked plants and flowers filled the air after their saturation from such a heavy downpour. She found herself drawn to the outbuilding again and made her way across the wet lawn and up to the door. The door was stiff and gave a protesting creak. She walked inside and searched for a light switch to test if it had electricity installed. Finding the switch on the far side of the room, she flicked it up, but nothing happened. She instinctively gazed upwards at the naked bulb hanging precariously from the ceiling. Perhaps it just needed replacing.

There was a lot of daylight pouring in through the large window that ran the whole length of the room. She stood with her hands on her hips looking around, trying to visualize what it once was. Maybe an art studio, with so much light it would have been perfect. Yet despite the sunlight, the room still felt extremely cold, and she shivered. The place was empty all bar a wicker chair that had seen better days, standing in the far corner and a large antique trunk next to it. Jen took a closer look. It was covered in dust. She tried the lid, but it wouldn't budge and then she noticed the lock. It was quite a big lock. The brass key in the kitchen drawer she had found the other day may fit. She dashed back outside and down the garden towards the house, but Alison stopped her in her tracks, standing in the kitchen ready to go.

"I'm starving. Can we go somewhere for lunch?" she asked eagerly. Jen stopped in her tracks and smiled meekly.

"Yes of course we can, darling." The trunk could wait until later, until Alison had gone. After all this was her last day with her and she would have all the time to investigate the trunk when she was gone.

Her heart was pounding as she ran up the road and then stopped just before the front door, gaining her breath, and then quickly wiping her tears away before running indoors.

"Esperanza is that you?" Dorothy called

out having heard the door slam. She smiled apologetically at Alfredo. "I'm so sorry."

"No problem. I can come back another day if it's more convenient?"

"No, please stay. I want to share my good news with her while you are here," she said. He nodded in agreement to wait. He had been longing to see Esperanza since the church fete.

Dorothy tapped on the bedroom door and then entered. She found Esperanza sitting on her bed. The room was small with nothing more than a neatly made single bed, a wardrobe and a small table and chair that she sat at to do her writing, scattered with paper and pencils. The window was open, and Jessica and Anna could be heard playing in the garden below.

"Espe, what on earth is the matter?" Dorothy walked across the room towards her. Esperanza looked up at her. "I don't want to leave," she sobbed. *Don't want to leave Carlos* was what she wanted to say but didn't dare.

"Oh sweetheart, then I have some very good news for you because we don't need to."

"What? Why?" Esperanza stared back at her in disbelief through her stinging tears. "I don't understand."

"Come downstairs, I will tell you everything in the presence of our visitor."

Esperanza looked worried. "Mama, look at me, I can't see anyone in this state, my eyes are all puffy."

"Go and wash your face, brush your hair and come straight down," she instructed, then gave a small reassuring smile. "Everything is going to be just fine, you'll see."

"You still haven't told me who the visitor is."

"You will find out as soon as you come downstairs." Dorothy left the room without another word.

Esperanza couldn't think who could possibly be waiting downstairs, and then suddenly she had an idea—could it be Carlos? Had he come round to apologise and meet her mother? No, she had never told him her address, unless he asked someone for it, but it still didn't explain her mother's change of heart about leaving, unless he had talked her out of it of course, but she doubted that very much.

As she entered the room Alfredo stood up and displayed a charming smile, clearly delighted to see her, although disappointingly to Alfredo, he could see the feeling was not mutual. If anything, Esperanza seemed disappointed to see him and confused as to what he was doing in her home drinking port with her mother. She had spotted the two crystal glasses and a decanter of port on the table in front of them.

"Hello Esperanza," he said, enamored by how pretty she looked, even prettier than he remembered.

"Hello again," she replied shyly.

"Esperanza," come and sit down. Her mother beckoned her to the spare armchair in front of them. "I have some exciting news. Alfredo's father has offered me a management position. I'm to run their new jewellery shop opening here in two weeks from now. All thanks to Alfredo of course, putting in a good word for me." She threw an appreciative smile Alfredo's way.

"I was very impressed with how your mother organised the church fete and thought she would be ideal for the position," Alfredo said.

"I see," Esperanza replied, trying to make sense of it all. "Would you not be running the shop yourself; I mean for your father?" She asked, looking inquisitively at Alfredo.

"I must oversee both shops, here and Santa Cruz and I can't be in two places at once." He smiled again.

She held his stare, wondering if he was sincere. "Does your father not run the one in Santa Cruz?"

"My father is of ill health now and does not spend much time in the shops, he takes care of the businesses behind the scenes."

"I see," she replied coolly. "But Mama who will look after Jessica and Anna after school and cook dinner?"

"Why, you, of course darling. It's not like you have anything else to do, other than write stories." There was a hint of sarcasm in Dorothy's tone.

"Do you write?" Alfredo seemed impressed.

"Yes. Someday I hope to become a published author."

"Alfredo you must come for supper next week, to let me say thank you properly." Dorothy interrupted, embarrassed by her daughter's dreamy expression, the one she always got when talking about writing.

Alfredo dragged his attention back to Dorothy. "I would be delighted to. I would also like to ask Esperanza if she would accompany me to a dinner party next week." His eyes fixed back on Esperanza's. "My cousin is holding a pre-wedding party in Santa Cruz. I must warn you though, it won't be exciting, he has to be the most boring person I know. You would be doing me a great favor if you came with me and prevent me from dying of boredom."

Dorothy let out an undeserving hoot of laughter.

Esperanza wriggled nervously in her seat. "Oh I don't think..."

"She would love to, wouldn't you darling?" Dorothy intercepted, flashing a pleading look Esperanza's way.

Esperanza held her mother's glare. How could she say no? He had offered her mother a job, saved them from going back to England. It was the right thing to do, to accept his invitation. She turned her attention to Alfredo. "I don't think it will be that boring, is what I was about to say," she said, and then glanced back at her mother, who was clearly relieved. "I'd be delighted to accompany you," she added politely.

"Great, that's settled then," Alfredo looked extremely pleased.

The door flung open taking them all by surprise as Jessica and Anna came bounding into the room like two playful puppies.

"Girls!" Dorothy raised her voice at them. "Show some manners and greet our guest properly. This is Mr Sanchez."

Alfredo stood up and held out his hand. Jessica was the first one to shake it.

"Hello," she said. Anna was about to shake and then looked down at her grubby hands, still dirty from digging in the soil earlier, searching for worms. "Sorry, dirty hands. I remember you though, from the church fete. You like Espe my sister." She giggled, remembering watching him from the church grounds, she never missed a trick. Esperanza turned the colour of scarlet and wriggled nervously again in her chair.

"Yes, I like Esperanza, I like you all," he replied tactfully in front of their mother, but knowing full well what Anna meant. And she was right. He did like Esperanza very much, he had not been able to stop thinking about her since they had met.

"Go and wash your hands, Anna," Dorothy reprimanded her. "I'm so sorry, Alfredo. Do you know, being in the shop will be a true delight to get away from these two monsters?"

Alfredo laughed. "We were all children

once."

"Indeed we were, but I don't remember being quite as badly behaved," she replied, finding him utterly charming. He was going to make the most wonderful son-in-law one day, if she got her way, which she invariably did. And now Esperanza had just agreed to go on a date with him, things were looking very positive.

Chapter Twelve

Thunderous swirls of deep purple and yellow mixed with dark grey clouds threatened a storm on its way. Seagulls shrieked, flocking inland away from the inevitable. She stood on the edge of a cliff top, behind her a subtropical garden took a battering in the wind. Her hand instinctively glided over her tiny stomach, contemplating ending her misery right there and then. But this was not just about her life, she had a responsibility to her unborn child. Coming to her senses she backed away from the cliff edge, suddenly startled by the electric, flashing light above her, followed by an almighty crash of thunder. She turned and fled through the rain that began lashing at her skin. While running to take cover, nearby rose bushes threw out their petals in a trail that seemed to follow her all the way to the outbuilding, courtesy of the wind.

The door was stiff. She pulled at it hard but still it would not give way. Sobbing and soaked to the bone, she tugged and banged at it with both her fists, using all her strength but still it would not budge.

Jen flung open her eyes, her heart racing and pounding in her chest. It took her a few minutes to realise that the banging she could still hear ringing in her ears was in fact now, a loud tapping on the glass pane of the kitchen door. She got up from the sofa and went towards the kitchen, trying to gain her composure and sweep the image of the distraught young woman in her dream from her mind. She was delighted to see Petra waiting the other side of the patio door.

"Petra, how was Germany?"

Petra stepped into the kitchen.

"Cold," she replied, giving a dramatized shiver. "I'm happy to be back." Petra was quick to notice the bleary look in Jen's eyes. "Sorry, did I disturb your siesta?"

"Oh no its fine. I dozed off on the sofa. I was up early this morning; I took Alison back to the airport."

"Alison, your daughter?"

"Yes, it was a lovely, unexpected visit. But now she's gone back."

"Oh how wonderful that she came to see you. What a shame I didn't meet her."

"She will be back soon, I'm sure. Coffee?"

"As long as I'm not intruding."

"Not at all. I was just going to make one."

Petra sat down at the kitchen table. "You said you took Alison to the airport. Do you have a car now?"

"No, I hired one when Alison was here." She glanced back over her shoulder, before reaching for the coffee mugs. "I think I will get a little runaround though; it's been very handy and saves walking up those monstrous hills."

Petra laughed. "Oh yes, indeed, couldn't agree more."

"So, tell me about Germany." Jen busied around the kitchen digging out some biscuits from the cupboard.

"I went to see my cousin, her husband died recently, all very sad. I caught up with a couple of friends. I swear I will never visit Germany again in the winter. I said it before, but I mean it this time. Minus three degrees it is far too cold."

"Oh my goodness, sounds like England in the winter. Well, the weather here has been a bit unsettled, we've had a lot of rain." She placed the coffee and biscuits on the table. "But thankfully not minus three degrees, more like eighteen degrees," she chuckled.

"Well, now that we have discussed the weather, do you have something more interesting to tell me?" Petra, smiled at Jen to soften what might have been considered by some as a curt reply.

Jen, oblivious, continued. "I've decided to turn the outbuilding into a studio apartment for holiday rentals," she announced.

"Excellent idea. It will give you a nice little income."

"I'm going to put a swimming pool in the garden and maybe offer some meals too if they want it."

"How exciting." Petra took a sip of coffee.

Jen grew pensive, not being able to shake the woman dressed in black from her mind, who now she believed to be the same woman she kept dreaming about. "Petra, have you ever seen or met a rather odd-looking woman here? By here, I mean in the garden, on these grounds?"

Petra frowned. "And by odd, you mean?"

"She wears black, old fashioned style of clothing, 1920's I would say."

Petra immediately nodded, knowing full well who Jen was referring to. "I wondered how long it would take before she showed herself again."

"I don't understand—showed herself?"

"Not everyone can see her, you are quite honoured." Petra frowned again. "Grace didn't see her, or at least I don't think she did, she never mentioned her to me."

"Who is she?"

"A lost soul I presume, trying to bring over a message. Trapped in time with no way out."

Jen leaned back in her chair; her face had suddenly lost its colour. She swallowed hard. "You mean she's a…"

"Ghost? Yes."

"But she can't be. I met her at the Mirador, she spoke to me. We had a conversation. It was real, very real."

Petra placed her coffee down and sat forward with intrigue. "What did she say to you?"

"I don't remember exactly. Philosophical chatter - life, decisions, she was most strange."

"Well, she would be," Petra displayed a watery smile.

"But no, it can't be right." Jen shook her head defiantly. "I don't even believe in ghosts. My parents always taught me they don't exist. My father said it was complete tosh."

"Tosh?" Petra looked blank.

"Rubbish, nonsense."

"To those nonbelievers I guess it is tosh," she replied indignantly, folding her arms and sitting back in her chair.

The sweet smell of honeysuckle and a potent aroma of damp soil after a recent sudden downpour filled the air as Alfredo and Esperanza walked along a narrow-cobbled street leading full circle back to Esperanza's home. He had purposely had them dropped off by car away from the house so that he could walk her back and spend some time alone. They had hardly spoken all evening.

Through no fault of their own, they had been seated apart, for which Alfredo was annoyed but hadn't wanted to cause a fuss in front of some very influential people. There had been so many people to speak to and poor Esperanza had sat quietly most of the evening, making polite conversation only when spoken to, which wasn't often. He could sense she was bored and on reflection he wished he had taken her somewhere else on their first date, somewhere where they could be alone and were able to talk.

"You are shivering," he took off his jacket and placed it around her shoulders."

"Oh thank you," she accepted his jacket without protest, glad of some warmth around her bare arms.

"I'm sorry that it wasn't a great evening to say the least but thank you for coming anyway." He gave a sideways glance at her, she was looking ahead, somewhat quiet, and preoccupied.

"It was um..." she had to think hard for the appropriate word to describe her experience this evening and then she said "interesting," for want of a better word.

"Interesting," he laughed. "It was many things, boring, tedious, pompous, but interesting isn't quite the word I would have chosen to describe my cousin's party."

She smiled shyly and their eyes met. He pulled her arm gently to stop her from walking. "I'm sorry it was a disastrous first date. Let me make it up to you, take you out for dinner tomorrow night. I know a lovely restaurant on the edge of town..." He stopped, noticing the unease in her eyes. "You don't want to, do you?"

"Yes, no, look it's not you. I'm just not sure I'm ready for this." Her thoughts were very much with Carlos this evening, as hard as she tried to dismiss him from her mind, but she couldn't help feeling guilty for going out with another man, despite Carlos having let her go now.

"Ready for this?" He frowned not grasping her meaning.

"Exactly, what is this? My mother seems to have thrown us together, she can be very persuasive."

Alfredo shook his head. "Your mother had nothing to do with me asking you out, I promise you. From the moment I met you at the church fete, I've not been able to get you out of my mind."

She blushed and looked away from his intense stare.

"But if you don't feel the same way, or..." A horrid thought suddenly crossed his mind. "Or if there's someone else..."

"No, there's not anyone else, not anymore," she replied. Her glum expression said it all.

"I see." It suddenly all made sense to Alfredo. "I think he broke your heart; he was a fool to have let you go."

"It's complicated and I'd rather not speak about it, if it's all the same." An unexpected smile appeared on her lips. "And it's time I put it behind me, so yes, I would love to go out for dinner tomorrow night."

"You would?" he was momentarily stunned by her sudden change of heart. "Wonderful. I'll pick you up at seven then."

They arrived at her house. She took his jacket from her shoulders and passed it back to him. "Thank you."

He smiled tenderly. She was so beautiful, he fought hard to resist the urge to kiss her, knowing full well it would scare her off if he moved too quickly, and he would also run the risk of her mother spotting them from the window. "Well, I will see you tomorrow then."

She nodded. "Yes, see you tomorrow." He walked away and she called out to him "Alfredo."

He turned around, looking pleased with himself.

"Thank you. It wasn't as bad as you think it was. I have had worse evenings with mother and her church cronies."

He laughed and she did too as she walked indoors.

"You seem happy, was it a lovely evening sweetheart?" Dorothy sat at the table sipping cocoa, she had been waiting patiently for Esperanza to come home and tell her all about her evening.

"Not exactly lovely, it was more your scene than mine."

"And what is that supposed to mean?" Dorothy replied, guardedly.

"Pompous," Esperanza said, remembering it had been one of Alfredo's choice descriptions of the party.

"Well, I expect there were a lot of important people there. The Sanchez family are very well respected and influential. And for the record, I'm not pompous," Dorothy added.

Esperanza rolled her eyes. "Any more cocoa?"

"Yes, sit down and I will get you some." She walked over to the stove and Esperanza flopped down on the chair. She pulled at the side of her dress, the fine broidery was digging into her ribs and was far too tight in certain areas owing to the fact the dress was two years old, although thankfully unnoticeable to others.

"When are you seeing him again?" Dorothy asked with bated breath.

"Tomorrow evening. He's taking me to a restaurant."

"Oh so soon, that's a good sign, how delightful." Dorothy's face had lit up at the news, carrying a cup of hot cocoa and placing it down on the table.

"So, do you get on well then?"

"I've no idea." Esperanza picked up the mug and blew at the steam, cautious not to burn her lips.

"What do you mean you have no idea? You've just spent the evening with him, surely you must know if you like him?" Dorothy quizzed.

"We weren't seated together; I hardly saw

him all evening."

"I see. Well, I'm sure you will have a lovely time tomorrow."

Esperanza nodded unconvinced. He wasn't Carlos, nothing like him. She had walked past the harbour quite a few times in recent weeks hoping to see him, but he was never there. She wondered if he had stopped coming to Tenerife altogether, and if she would ever see him again. He probably thought she had already left for England. If he knew she was going out on dates with someone else, he would without doubt be hurt.

"I don't know if I should go tomorrow," she said, her thoughts now back on Carlos.

"Now you listen to me, young lady." Dorothy stared at her, wagging her finger at Esperanza from across the table. "Alfredo is a decent and lovely man from a good family. You are truly blessed that he has shown an interest in you. Don't you dare embarrass me or our good name by giving him the run around."

"I'm not giving him the run around. Mother, surely I should be able to choose who I see?"

"I can assure you that you will not find anyone better here in Puerto de la Cruz," she continued, not answering Esperanza's question. "You have agreed to go out with him, and you will go on that date tomorrow night. Do you hear me?"

"Yes Mama," she sighed wearily.

What was the point of arguing with her, she would never win?

"Good, now drink your cocoa, it's late, we need to go to bed. And you need to look fresh for tomorrow evening."

Jen sat on the cold stone floor of the outbuilding with a few possible keys scattered around her to fit the treasure trunk. She tried three without success and it was the fourth one she got lucky with. She lifted the heavy lid and peered inside. Blankets. Crocheted blankets. She picked one up and studied its impeccably artistic stitching.

Life is full of curiosities.

She dropped the blanket and turned around. Then realising the words must have come from her own mind, she delved her hand back inside and felt something hard at the bottom of the pile. She pushed back a beige crocheted blanket, revealing a brown leather book. There was no title, no author's name, no writing on the cover at all. She opened the book carefully, the cream coloured pages, worn with time, were fragile, and the scrawly handwriting was hard to read, but nevertheless she tried...

All she could feel was emptiness, loneliness, a sense of loss—loss of her freedom, loss of the chance to ever be happy in love. An impossible situation for which there was no way out, no way to seek real love or happiness ever again. Marriage is for life, for better or for worse, in sickness and in health, for richer or poorer, and she was about to solemnly declare these vows that would tie her down like shackles to a sinking ship.

Jen sat with her back resting against the trunk. Her eyebrows met in a deep frown. These words were so incredibly sad. Were they a real account of an unwanted marriage or fictional she wondered? It was written in third person which would indicate it being a story not about the author, but was it based on real events? Intrigued, she flicked ahead stopping at approximately ten pages in...

She lay in bed. The only light a solitary candle flickering wildly, courtesy of the breeze coming in from the open window, its shadow casting erratic dark silhouettes on the wall, and on the ceiling above. The familiar sound of the door handle squeaking as he walked into the room, forced her to slide further under the sheets. His boots echoed crossing the wooden floor towards her. The bed went down heavily on one side with a creak as he sat down, stripping one by one, each item of his clothing, throwing them into a heap on the floor. He slipped under the sheets next to her, his touch cold against her warm skin. She turned on her side, away from him, trying to contain her quivering body - not from excitement or delight, but from fear that he would take her again, and again, forcefully and against her will as he so often did. He moved closer, sliding his hand over her shoulder, under her arm, groping at her breasts. She could feel him becoming aroused. And that meant one thing, there would be no escaping her marital duty this evening!

Jen let out a big, heavy sigh, wanting to read more but feeling uncomfortably stiff still sitting on the cold floor. She stood up and decided to take the book back to the house. Tonight she would read it enjoying a glass of wine or two. Although it was a difficult read, she couldn't help but want to know more and if there would be a happy outcome. The author, whoever they were, had certainly painted a very bleak and disturbing picture of marriage so far. She pulled the lid down on the trunk but didn't see the need to lock it, after all there were only old blankets inside. And she wondered why it had been locked in the first place, perhaps because of the book? Maybe it was valuable to someone once. Lost in thought about her newfound prized possession, she strode across the lawn, unaware of the pale, shadowed face in the window behind her, watching her every move.

The restaurant was small and intermit, soft lighting and cosy tables with checkered red and white cloths. Esperanza and Alfredo sat at a table close to the window. The view, although it was now dusk, was undoubtedly stunning, looking over the sea and the volcanic coastline from its prime elevated position.

"Thank you, but I couldn't eat another thing," Esperanza replied to the waiter who had just offered her the dessert menu.

"Coffee?" Alfredo suggested eagerly, not wanting the evening to finish yet.

She didn't wish to appear rude and therefore nodded her head in agreement.

"Are you excited about the new shop?" She asked, trying to keep the conversation flowing. There had been quite a few awkward moments when neither of them knew what to speak about. Although Alfredo seemed less bothered than she about the lack of topics to discuss, and simply tucked into his meal, enjoying the food and happy to be seen out with such a pretty, young girl.

"Yes, but probably not as much as your mother is," he replied, with amusement in his eyes.

"I know, she has been talking about it rather a lot. I think she is looking forward to having something new to do—a purpose in life again."

"It could not have been easy for her, bringing up three children alone," Alfredo acknowledged pensively.

"No, it wasn't."

He noticed the forlorn expression in Esperanza's eyes. "Sorry, I didn't mean to make you feel uncomfortable."

"It's fine. I was just thinking about my father, that's all—I miss him," she exclaimed, trying to keep her tears at bay.

"Of course you do." He reached out and touched her hand.

"I think it was probably worse for my sisters," she admitted, putting on a brave face. "They were so young and found it hard to understand, Anna in particular. I comforted her night after night. Mother was too upset to be of any use to her, she, herself, spent hours in her bedroom crying. Jessica was quiet and hid her feelings away as she always does, but Anna relied on me, which meant I had to be strong, and it also meant I didn't have much time to grieve myself."

The waiter placed two coffees down in front of them and made a swift exit, sensing they were having the type of conversation that shouldn't be disturbed.

Alfredo smiled warmly. "If you don't mind me saying so, I think you would make an excellent mother one day. And wife," he added.

She blushed, not really understanding why he should say that. Was it just a simple observation or did he have intentions of her being *his* wife and mother to *his* children one day? That was what her mother hoped for, she had made that quite clear, but not something Esperanza had considered yet, after all, this was only their first proper date. She sipped her coffee, and he did too; his eyes firmly still fixed on hers with each sip. And then another awkward silence bestowed them once more.

Chapter Thirteen

It is better to have loved and lost than to have never loved at all!
Alfred Lord Tennyson – 1850.

This is a matter of opinion, for if one had not loved, then one would not have known endured heartache and the pain of loss that comes with love itself. Perhaps it is best to have never loved at all, contrary to Alfred Lord Tennyson's proverb!

Jen looked up from the book, now sitting comfortably of the sofa with a glass of red wine in her other hand. She contemplated the author's words. Maybe she was right, thinking about David and her own disappointment in love. She suspected the author to be female now. And it was clear that she was no stranger to heartache. These strong words were full of emotion, sadness mainly. She frowned trying to understand the following lines, but the writing had become even more scrawly, and the pages faded, so she turned the pages until she could find one that was comprehendible.

It was a risk, the biggest risk but she had to take it. She had to see him, if not for one last time. Like an addictive drug she had succumbed to him. A love so genuine, pure, and perfect, unlike her marriage, which was quite the contrary, based on practicalities, convenience, false pretenses, no love—there had never been love—maybe fondness once upon a time, but that had all diminished, gone in a puff of smoke. And all that was left was the promise of hope. Hope was all she had left to hold onto.

Gosh! Jen said out loud, realising that whoever this story was about, not only was she in a very unhappy marriage, but she was also having an affair. Just then Jen's mobile rang. She placed the book down and picked up her phone, stopping it from vibrating all around the coffee table.

"Hi Jen." Kate's cheerful voice echoed down the line.

"Kate. How are you?"

"I'm fine. Just wanted to let you know that your boxes were picked up today and should be with you by the end of next week."

"Oh thank you so much. I'm sorry to have put you through all this trouble, packing my things and arranging for them to be sent to me, I feel terribly guilty."

"It's fine, honestly. It was a bit cloak and dagger going into the house, which is not me at all, but it was actually quite fun, sweet revenge on your part." She grinned down the phone. "Have you heard from him?"

"David, yes. He texted me a few days ago saying if I wasn't home by the end of the month he would be filing for a divorce under the grounds of neglect."

"Neglect? As if! He cheated on you, what a cheek he has. Surely he knew you wouldn't be back after we emptied the house?"

"He can be slow on the uptake at times. I told him don't bother waiting until the end of the month, just file for it now and not under neglect but adultery on your part."

"And what did he say to that?"

"Nothing, he didn't reply."

"Typical. I saw him only two days ago with *her*. They were going into Tesco's when I was just pulling out of the carpark."

"That's what I mean, Kate. What exactly is he planning to do with her, if I was stupid enough to come back at the end of the month?"

"I know, it's crazy. Anyway, how's things over there in sunny Tenerife?"

"Great. Alison came over as you know, we spent a few quality days together—oh and I've decided what I want to do here—I'm going to turn the outbuilding into a self-contained studio and also put in a swimming pool."

"Oh wow! That will be great. I'm so happy for you, Jen. We all miss you at school, but I think you are doing the right thing."

They chatted for a while longer and then Kate had to go. "Let me know when your boxes arrive."

"Will do and thanks again, Kate. Speak soon."

Placing her mobile back down on the table, she noticed the local newspaper and the classified section on the back. She picked it up and skimmed through some adverts stopping at C.G. Constructions. She read the advert with interest and checked her watch. It was almost 6pm, they could still be open. She dialed the number shown, hoping they would speak English; to her relief the young woman who answered the phone did. She was polite and helpful and said she would send someone over tomorrow to give a quote for both the studio and the pool.

Jen hung up with a smile, feeling pleased she had taken the first step to starting her new adventure.

Noticing her glass was almost empty she went to the kitchen to get a refill, and suddenly stopped in her tracks, as a dark figure walked past the glass doors in the garden. She rushed towards the doors and pulled them open, stepping out onto the cold tiles. But there was no one there. She dashed further into the garden, now standing on the lawn. Still no sign of anyone.

Jennifer, pull yourself together!

"It's your stupid imagination again," she chided out loud.

Chapter Fourteen

The lighting was set perfectly, designed to catch the eye. Each glass covered counter had its own soft glowing lamp that shone on a collection of stunning jewels—sapphires, diamonds, rubies, pearls in every form of jewellery such as rings, necklaces, earrings, and bracelets. Then the less expensive range, although still high end, boasting a range of costume jewellery, including fashionable head pieces, hair combs and slides, handmade filigree brooches and more. The little shop was packed both inside and out. Dorothy was in her element showing everyone around for the grand opening of Joyeria De Sanchez. She handed out brochures, which she had studied no end, and knew exactly what each piece of jewellery was made from and where it had originated from. Dressed to impress she looked glamorous in a cream satin frock and her hair fashionably curled only at that back and sides, straight on top. She certainly had some male attention this evening, but she was far too busy to notice.

Esperanza watched her mother from outside of the shop. She looked younger, happier than she had seen her in years, and she was pleased for her.

"Espe, can we have an orange juice?" Anna bounced around the corner with Jessica in tow. They were both wearing matching pink dresses, much to Jessica's horror of not wanting to be dressed in matching clothes with her younger sister.

"Yes, wait there." Esperanza made her way through a crowd chatting at the entrance, making her excuses politely until she reached the table of drinks.

"Ah there you are." Alfredo crept up behind her and placed his hand on her arm. "Are you enjoying the grand opening?" he smiled broadly, proud of the shop and happy to see her.

"Um yes, of course." She smiled politely.

He leaned in closer to her ear. "It's OK, I know it's dreadfully boring, a bit like cousin, David's party."

"Not quite as boring at that," she smirked.

"How about we escape and go for a walk?" he suggested.

She turned to face him with two glasses of orange juice in her hands. *No, let's not,* she wanted to say, but instead found herself agreeing.

"Yes, alright." After all he had been kind enough to give her mother a job and save them from poverty, she owed it to her mother if nothing else. And he had taken her out for dinner, which was also kind.

"Are you going to drink both of those?" He asked.

She giggled at his expression of disbelief. "Oh no, these are for my sisters." Sometimes he was funny, she had to admit. He wasn't all that bad; it was just that they had little in common.

"Meet me around the corner in five minutes." He pointed to the little side street next to the shop.

It took nearly five minutes for Esperanza to find her sisters but after giving them both their drinks and warning Anna not to wander off and after asking Jessica to keep a close eye on her, she finally slipped away to meet Alfredo, who was waiting patiently for her at the agreed spot.

"You are my saviour." He placed a gentle hand of her back, leading her out of sight.

"I don't think my mother would even notice me gone, she's so busy."

"Yes, she's enjoying herself. I think she will love working at the shop."

Esperanza agreed with a nod. "How come your father isn't here tonight?" she asked with interest.

"Sadly, he's unwell again."

"Oh I'm sorry to hear that, nothing serious I hope."

"No, yes—well it's complicated." Alfredo lifted his hat to a gentleman on the other side of the road in greeting. She couldn't help but notice he looked dapper this evening in a tailored pinned stripped suit with a white silk handkerchief poking from his top pocket. He was always immaculately dressed, but this evening even more so for the opening.

"I'm sorry, I didn't mean to pry." She could sense his unease at her question.

"No, it's fine, you didn't pry. He has influenza but he also has lung cancer. It's just that no one knows about the cancer. Only us, his family. He doesn't like people making a fuss, he's a proud man."

"Alfredo, that's awful." Esperanza looked aghast, not expecting such shocking news.

"I know. To be honest, I feel quite useless."

"No, you mustn't think like that. You are not useless at all. You are here at the opening, you arranged it all and you manage his other shops."

Alfredo pursed his lips and nodded. "I have to, he's simply not well enough."

They reached the top of the road and turned into Plaza Del Charco, lined with palm trees, flowers with dotted pretty little bars and restaurants. They sat down on a grey stone wall.

"How long does..." she stopped mid flow, maybe she shouldn't ask that question. It was hurtful to ask how long his father had left to live and she could see the deep sadness in Alfredo's eyes.

"How long does...?" he repeated, waiting for

her to finish her question, unaware of what she was about to ask.

"How long does it take to pluck a chicken or goose?" She said in all seriousness, and he burst out laughing so loudly that people sitting in a bar opposite them stared over with surprise.

"That's what I love about you—your ability to make me laugh when you don't even try. Why on earth would you wish to know that?"

"For a story I'm writing," she replied.

My main character is given a chicken as a gift, or it might be a goose, I haven't quite decided yet but anyway she has no idea how to prepare it for cooking."

"When are you going to let me read your work?" he asked, bumping shoulders with her affectionately.

"Never, probably," she giggled.

He loved it when she giggled, laughed, or just even smiled. She looked so radiant, so very, beautiful and the more time he spent with her, the more he fell in love with her.

"Well, if you become a published author then you will need to let people read your stories."

He was not the first person to tell her that, she remembered Carlos saying the same thing.

He noticed the sadness in her eyes. "I'm sorry, I didn't mean to upset you."

"No, you are right, I do need to let people read my work. I'm just worried it's not good enough, that's all."

"I'd like to think you trust my opinion, my judgement," he frowned at her.

"Oh I do, absolutely."

"Then maybe soon you will let me read what happened to the woman who needed to pluck a chicken, or a goose, even."

Esperanza let out an unexpected hoot of laughter taking Alfredo by surprise, and the people across in the bar opposite again. He then joined in with her infectious laughter. The more they laughed the funnier it became until eventually they were doubled up with hysteria. Finally, Esperanza rested her weary head from laughing on his shoulder. He glided a hand over her silky long dark hair. Surprisingly, his touch felt good, even comforting in an odd sort of way, although she had no idea why. She sat up straight and looked at him. His eyes were kind, and she realised that she might actually have some kind of feelings for him after all, although what they were, she was unsure. It wasn't like the feelings she had when she was with Carlos, no butterflies in her tummy or flutters of excitement in her heart but more of a feeling of being warm and safe. He leaned forward and their lips touched. His kiss was soft and tender and to her surprise again she enjoyed it.

"You have no idea how long I have wanted to do that," he admitted to her. "Since the moment I first met you."

She blushed and stood up from the wall. He followed her and placed an arm around her shoulders as they walked back up the road towards the shop. She knew she must forget about Carlos. He was her first love and always would be, but he had let her go and she felt quite sure that he was not coming back. The words of Alfred Lord Tennyson sprang to mind, and she made a mental note to add it to one of her stories one day.

It is better to have loved and lost than to have never loved at all!

Tonight, she had kissed Alfredo, this changed everything now.

Chapter Fifteen

He opened the small gate that gave an intrusive squeak as he closed it behind himself and walked up the path towards the green, wooden front door. He spotted the chipped floral name plate that read *Villa Esperanza* and above it an old rusty bell that had seen better days. It felt surreal standing there on the doorstep, as if coming home after an awfully long time away, yet he had never stepped foot in the house before.

A love like no other. A love that will never be forgotten.

Why on earth would he have thought that? Puzzled by the strange words that seemed to have popped into his head as if from nowhere, he rapped his knuckles on the wood of the door, not trusting the bell would survive it if he pulled its corroded chain. A moment later the door opened.

"Carlos! " Jen was as surprised to see him as he was to see her.

"How did you know where I live?"

"My secretary gave me your address," he replied sounding a little confused. "C.G Constructions."

"Oh. You work for C.G Constructions?"

"Kind of, I'm the owner," he replied, wryly.

She smacked her forehead with the palm of her hand, feeling a complete fool for not working out his initials.

"Of course, C.G. Carlos Garcia. Come in, Carlos, I'm so sorry." She opened the door wider, and he stepped inside. She led him into the living room.

"This is a nice surprise. I didn't make the connection with the name Mrs Brown," he said, standing before her with his clipboard in hand.

She twiddled her hair nervously. Why had she given the name Mrs Brown to his secretary, her marriage was over, she really needed to stop using the name Brown and go back to her maiden name of Williams. "Yes, force of habit. Brown is my married name, which I should stop using seeing as my marriage is over."

"So, you bought this villa recently?" he asked, sensing she felt uncomfortable and thinking he should get on with the reason why he was there.

"Not exactly bought it." She cleared her throat with a small nervous cough.

"Oh, if you rent, you would need the

owner's permission before doing any work," he said in earnest.

"No, um, you don't understand. I am the owner," she confirmed, feeling as flustered as she sounded for some unknown reason. Was it because he was so extremely handsome or just that he had taken her by surprise with him being the owner of the construction company? Either way, she needed to get a grip and fast. "This villa was left to me by a good friend. I inherited it," she explained.

"Oh," he looked taken aback. "Must have been an incredibly good friend. I'm sorry for your loss."

"Yes, she was. Look, sorry, I expect you want to see the outbuilding—shall we?" She pointed in the direction of the kitchen which led to the garden.

"Yes sure." He sensed her unease again and simply agreed without saying any more on the subject of her friend. Letting her lead the way, he followed through to the kitchen and then into the garden.

"You have a beautiful garden. Do you have a gardener?" He glanced around admiring the stunning views of the coast below.

"Yes, I inherited him too. He comes around once a week, he does all the gardens in this street, so I believe." She walked a couple of yards forward and pointed to the lawn. "I'd like the pool around here."

Some of the most beautiful things in the world cannot be seen or heard but only felt from the heart.

She cleared her throat with another small nervous cough after hearing those random words again. She had spent too much time reading that damn book. Unwittingly, sayings about love popping into her head were starting to become the norm, much to her dismay. And fancying a man she hardly knew was not normal behaviour either.

"Sorry, uh, what did you say?" Carlos frowned, staring back at her confused.

Realising that there was a chance that she may have said those words out loud, she blushed profusely and wished the ground would swallow her up.

"I said—I said I would like the pool about here." She pointed again, glazing over what may or may not have just happened, as she was still unsure if she had actually said those words out loud. That was the problem, it was hard to determine where they came from. Perhaps he had heard them too?

It was at least half an hour later by the time Carlos had finished measuring the outbuilding and talking to Jen about her ideas. He made notes and said he would get a quote to her hopefully by the next day.

"Would you like a coffee?" She asked, not wanting him to leave now, despite the cumbersome start of their appointment. It could get lonely at times living alone and not working, although Petra popped around quite regularly, but she realised just how much she missed having company.

He checked his watch.

"Sorry, if you need to get back to work, it's fine. I don't want to hold you up."

"No one is ever in a rush to get back to work," he joked. "I would love a coffee." He smiled that smile again, the one that made her feel like a love-struck teenager. She pushed a stray lock of hair from her right eye, looking pleased that he could stay longer. He followed her into the kitchen and sat down at the table while she made the coffee.

"You speak good English," she complimented him, glancing back at him over her shoulder. "Where did you learn?"

"From many English clients over the years." He noticed her hovering with the milk and sugar in her hands. "Just a little milk and one sugar please."

She returned his smile and then after adding the milk and sugar she handed him a mug before collecting her own.

"How's your son?" she asked, remembering he had spoken about him previously in the bar the other night.

"Oh very well, thank you. Back at university now."

"And Alison, your daughter?" he enquired.

"Same. I miss her very much. I expect you and your wife must miss your son too when he is away." She glanced at his wedding ring, taking a sip of coffee. She hadn't noticed it before in the bar. Good looking men were always married, either that or gay, she mused waiting for his response.

His face clouded with sadness. "My wife passed away three years ago—bowl cancer."

"Oh, I'm so sorry." She felt guilty now for mentioning his wife and for her own silly, selfish reasons, just to pry, just to find out if he was still married. She felt ashamed. What was happening to her?

Shame, guilt, is there really a difference in these destructive emotions?

"You were not to know." He surveyed the room, it had a pleasant atmosphere, cosy and lived-in, quite the contrary to what he had imagined. "I can't believe I'm actually sitting here in Villa Esperanza," he admitted.

Jen dragged her attention away from the words she had just heard. "Why?" she asked.

"My father spoke about this villa every time we came to La Paz. It was his father—my grandfather—that told him the story, after they had left La Gomera and settled here in Tenerife. I don't know how he found out this was the villa she lived in."

Jen stared back at him blankly. "What story? Sorry, who are you speaking about?"

"The story about Esperanza Sanchez."

"Esperanza Sanchez? Oh, is that someone who lived here in the past?" She could feel her curiosity rising. "Is that why this villa is called Villa Esperanza?"

"Yes," it's named after her, my

grandfather's first love.

Love knows no boundaries. It will always find you in the most unlikely of places. You can run from it but never hide.

She brushed the words quickly from her mind. Probably another line her subconscious had picked up from that book. The book! Maybe it had belonged to Esperanza. Before she could say anything, Carlos continued.

"The story is," he began, placing his coffee mug down on the table. "My grandfather was in love with her—Esperanza—but she tragically died, fell over the edge of the cliff in this back garden, apparently." He pointed to the huge, mature sturdy hedge that framed the garden from the cliff. It was hard to imagine anyone falling through it or over it for that matter, it was so big. "But not everyone believes it. They say it could have been suicide or that she was pushed."

"Gosh!" Jen sat back in her chair absorbing the story. She wanted to tell him about the book but decided against it. She would like to read it all first and determine if it was in any way related to the woman he was speaking about. It could be possible as many of the things written seemed so sad and tragic. She also wanted to tell him about the eccentric woman wearing black she had seen; the woman Petra called a ghost. But she felt foolish to speak about ghosts, especially to someone educated like Carlos who probably didn't believe in them either, just like herself.

"The villa was left empty for many years. No one around here wanted to buy it. They believed it to be bad luck, cursed or even haunted." He gave a small incredulous laugh and reached out and patted her hand. "It's all, how do you say?... Nonsense. Not like she died here in this house; it was outside."

Jen's eyes stared back at him wildly and he suddenly felt guilty for scaring her.

"It being bad luck to live here or being haunted is rubbish, you do know that, don't you? This is a lovely villa." He threw his right arm out showing it off to her. "Lovely," he said again, as if he had to convince her further.

"Yes, I know. Of course I know it's not true. I'm not superstitious, neither do I believe in ghosts," she retorted. "And as for luck, well, we create our own luck in this world."

"Absolutely, and I'm sure your friend's death had nothing to do with bad luck from living here," he said, with a reassuring pat on her hand again.

She had not even considered Grace's death could be anything to do with the villa—of course it couldn't have. Could it?

She pulled her hand away from his abruptly. "Thank you for coming." She stood up knocking the table which spilt her coffee cup. She grabbed the mug and placed it up right again. A little coffee trickled across the table and onto the floor. In a sequence of a few brisk moves, she grabbed a piece of kitchen roll from the work top, cleaned it up, and threw it in the bin, clearly flustered by the possibility of Grace's death being connected to a curse or bad omen from the villa.

"Oh, yes I should go." He had upset her now; he could see that. Why had been so stupid to tell her his grandfather's story? Not only could it have cost him a job if she turned it down, but he also liked her, he liked her very much and didn't wish to fall out with her over some silly rumours about the house and something so trivial that happened a lifetime ago.

She escorted him to the front door.

"I'm sorry if I upset you. My secretary will contact you tomorrow," he said apologetically.

"Thank you." She closed the door and sighed heavily leaning against the wood, relieved that he had gone but regretting she had practically thrown the poor man out. Maybe she had overreacted, just a tad, but he had been a little insensitive about Grace's death, although she was responsible for her own thoughts. *'Oh Men!'* She said out loud, walking back into the kitchen, feeling guilty now for overreacting.

She cleaned up the coffee cups, then poured herself an ice cold rose wine from the fridge.

With her thoughts now back on the book, she wandered back into the living room to find it, curious to find out if it was about Esperanza Sanchez. Making herself comfortable on the sofa she began to read...

The perfume of the sea engulfed them. The wind had become an orchestral conductor of the waves that cascaded over the rocks, crashing like thunder and rolling like lovers entwined together...

Chapter Sixteen

It had been four months since the opening of Joyeria De Sanchez and three and a half months since the death of Alfredo's father, leaving Alfredo the sole heir to all his jewellery shops—two in Tenerife, one in Gran Canaria and three on the mainland. Esperanza and Alfredo had become closer during these past few months. Alfredo had leaned on Esperanza for emotional support after his father's death and she had been there for him when he needed her most. The bond between them had grown immensely and so it felt right to Esperanza to accept Alfredo's proposal of marriage.

"Oh my goodness, I'm thrilled for you both!" Dorothy shrieked with excitement. Esperanza held out her hand in front of her mother, showing off her exquisite ring. Alfredo stood next to her beaming, positively pleased with himself at not only picking the perfect wife but the perfect ring too, a white gold band with a breathtaking Art Deco geometric diamond that couldn't fail to impress—simply elegant and magnificent all at once, as one would expect from the owner of a chain of high-quality jewellery shops.

"Oh I couldn't be happier," Dorothy wiped away her tears of joy and hugged her daughter.

Esperanza loved her ring, it shined from every angle and for the first time since she and Alfredo had met, she had butterflies in her tummy at the thought of getting married, the same excitement she had experienced whenever she had seen Carlos. But Carlos was in the past now, she had not seen or heard from him since the day they had argued, when he'd believed it right that she should move to England with her family.

Alfredo placed a strong arm around her shoulders, she felt a warm fuzzy feeling of contentment and joy looking up at him—her husband to be!

Diamonds are a girl's best friend! She had never felt so excited as she did on that fateful day when he proposed to her, when he snapped open that little black box and showed her the most beautiful ring she had ever seen,

and placed it on her finger. Little did she know what lay ahead...

What laid ahead? Jen bit her bottom lip, fully engrossed. The sudden vibration on the coffee table forced her to reach for her mobile phone and check her messages, it was Alison asking how she was and if she had started work on the outbuilding yet. She sent a quick reply saying she was waiting for a quote and promised to call her soon. And as she placed her phone back down on the table, a loud crash came from one of the bedrooms. It sounded like something had fallen over and smashed. She went into her own bedroom first, all looked fine—the bed was neatly made up with her dressing gown neatly laid out on the end, the wardrobe doors were closed, drawers with a photo of Alison, perfume and jewellery on top all looked the same as it always did, the room was just as she had left it. Then she checked the bathroom, nothing amiss there, only Gary the gecko sitting on the mirror, she sighed and rolled her eyes at him. That left Grace's bedroom. It was the only room she had still not ventured into. It was on her list having managed to clear out the drawers and cupboards in other parts of the house, but she had not yet plucked up the courage to enter Grace's room. She slowly pushed open the door and walked into the centre of the room. It was cold, extremely cold. The bed was neatly made up as it had been since

Grace left it that way on the day she died. Her fluffy slippers were still by the side of the bed. The dressing table was full of clutter, make up, perfume, earrings, brush and comb with Grace's dark hair entwined in them both. She walked into the bathroom en-suite, catching a glimpse of herself in the mirror and noticing tears were rolling down her cheeks. Oh Grace. She still found it hard to believe she was gone and would never be back.

The loss of a loved one can never be healed.

She spun around. Someone had spoken—a female voice. This time she knew without any doubt that it was not her own. But no one else was there, it didn't make sense. Perhaps an auditory hallucination. Oh gosh you are going insane, Jennifer, pull yourself together! And then she remembered the reason why she was standing in Grace's bedroom—the noise, what had caused the crashing sound?

Crashing like thunder and rolling like lovers, entwined together...

A sudden loud knock at the door made her jump almost out of her skin. She took a deep breath to calm her nerves and then dashed down the long hallway, pulling open the heavy old door to reveal a huge bouquet of flowers on the doorstep. She bent down and picked them up, peering right, then left to see who had left them but there was no one there. The little gate was closed at the end of the path. Glancing down at the flowers again she spotted a small white envelope wedged between some pink chrysanthemums and yellow roses, and so she opened it.

Please accept my apologies for yesterday and let me take you for dinner tomorrow evening, 7pm at Pedro's. C.G xx

From a distance she heard her mobile phone vibrate in the living room and so she dashed through and grabbed it from the sofa.

I hope you like the flowers. I am truly sorry. Look forward to seeing you tomorrow night xx

She smiled broadly, feeling like an excited teenager being asked out on a date. It was a date; she was actually going on a date tomorrow night and ... she inhaled the scent of the bouquet in her arms.... not only was he a handsome date, but he had sent her flowers too! She couldn't remember the last time David had sent her flowers, if ever. Carlos was without doubt a romantic.

Love doesn't need to be perfect; it just needs to be true. It is like a flower; give it attention and it will bloom!

Jen sighed wistfully, this time the words didn't bother her. She took the flowers into the kitchen to find a vase.

She held out her hand to admire her ring again. It made her feel special and grown up. She wasn't a young girl anymore; she was a young woman soon to be married. They had set the wedding date – 2nd of June and it was only two months away.

"Espe, here's some money. Buy us some meat—beef or chicken, your choice. You will have to cook it though as I won't be back on time, Jessica and Anna will be too hungry to wait for me to get back." Dorothy placed a last pin in the side of her curls and gave it a little pat of perfection, examining her work of art in the mirror.

"Meat again? We had meat last night," Esperanza said, watching her mother titivate herself ready for work.

"Well buy some fish then, I don't know."

"Mama, what will you do when I am married? Who will cook for you then?"

"I will hire a housekeeper of course; I just need to finish paying off our depts. A few more weeks and I will be able to. At least we now have a tutor for your sisters." She felt pleased at the prospect of being debt free all thanks to her well-paid job at Joyeria De

Sanchez. "And I'm quite sure Alfredo will have a housekeeper for you too. Have you found a home yet? Time is ticking, it's not long to the wedding."

Esperanza sighed. "No. Alfredo keeps showing me mansions. I don't want to live in a big old creepy house full of ghosts."

Dorothy guffawed. "Oh my dear girl, ghosts don't exist, and you should thank your lucky stars that you can live like a princess in a mansion, many would wish for your life. You have landed on your feet with Alfredo, you will never want for anything."

The fish market near the harbour was buzzing as always. Fishing boats bobbed in and out followed by flocks of seagulls, their shrills competing against the noise of the fishwives calling out the daily catch. Esperanza started to make her way towards the gathering crowds and then stopped abruptly at the sound of her name being called from behind. Her heart skipped a beat. She recognised his voice immediately. Not having time to think further she found herself turning around to face Carlos standing before her. As usual he had a fishing rod in one hand and a bucket in another. He seemed taller than she had remembered and in the sunlight his chestnut-coloured hair had an auburn tinge, which she had also never noticed before.

"Espe, what are you doing here? I thought you were in England?"

She cleared her throat with a small cough and nervously hid her left hand behind her back.

"We didn't go. We were meant to go, as you know and...well... mother was offered a job and we could stay after all." She forced a small smile, trying still to hide her nerves at seeing him after all this time and trying to ignore how handsome he looked with his sun kissed skin from working outside, his big strong arms and his tousled boyish hairstyle. She shuffled her feet on the spot. "I looked for you, here at the harbour, many times," she said, not looking him in the eyes, annoyed at herself for sounding pathetic. He had told her to go, he didn't want her, she reminded herself of that fact but still there she was admitting she had looked for him and had somehow forgiven him.

"I've not been here much. My mother has been sick. Father wanted me to stay home with her whenever he came here."

"Sorry to hear that, how is she now?"

"Much better." He eyed her closely. She looked even prettier than he remembered. He had missed her so much and thought about her often, wondering and imagining how her life was in England and above all wishing that she were happy with her new life.

"You are not buying fish, are you?" He pointed to the crowd ahead of them in amusement.

"Um, yes, for supper," she admitted, still holding her hand behind her back.

A grin crept across his face. "Why buy fish when there are plenty for free in the sea? Come on, my father won't be back for a while, let's catch you some supper." He walked off, expecting her to follow. Panicking she slipped her ring off her finger and into her pocket then ran after him.

"We really don't have to do this you know," she called out to him.

"Of course we do, you need supper," he shouted over the noise of the crowd.

Oh goodness, what if someone saw her? This was all a big mistake. She had to tell him about Alfredo, about her engagement.

"Here," he said, pointing to the wall where they used to sit.

"I think over there is better," she pointed further up the wall, in enough distance from the harbour and therefore less likely to be seen.

"What's wrong with here?" he frowned.

She marched further up the wall and sat down, not giving him the chance to question her decision any further.

"Do you remember what I taught you?" He handed her the rod and opened a small box that was in the bucket and took out some bait. Once attached, he said, "Alright, remember how to cast off?"

She tried but made a mess of it due to her anxiousness of being in his presence again and the chance of being spotted by someone who knew her or Alfredo. The rod fell out of her hand and into the sea beneath them. He rolled his eyes.

"Espe!" He laid on his stomach on the wall and grabbed the rod before it drifted away. He then walked behind her. "Stand up." He moved in closer and placed his hands over hers. She could feel the warmth of his body and his breath on her neck. She swallowed hard trying her best to concentrate but all she could think about was how much she yearned for him to kiss her, just like he used to.

"There, now we can sit down."

He sat down next to her on the wall again. There was a moment of uncomfortable silence, neither of them knowing quite what to say, she being worried about how to tell him she was engaged, and he being overwhelmed at seeing her and finding out she hadn't moved to England. But eventually they both spoke at the same time.

"No, you first," he offered politely.

"I...eh..." Oh God this was impossible. She couldn't find the words, not yet. "How have you been?" she asked, instead of telling him her news.

"I've missed you," he said, and she could tell by the look in his eyes. His arm brushed against hers and she longed for him even more.

"I've missed you too," she replied without thinking, without considering how this could ever lead anywhere now that she was engaged to Alfredo.

"I'm sorry, Espe." He pushed back a lose

strand of hair that had slipped over her left eye.

"Sorry for what?" she asked, blushing at his touch.

"For letting you go, for hurting you."

His eyes seemed to pour into her soul and all she wanted was for him to hold her tightly and kiss her again.

"It's fine," she replied, chiding herself inwardly. She was engaged and it was not right to think of another man in such an inappropriate way.

"It's not fine. I let you go because I thought you deserved more, but I didn't think about what you wanted. I didn't even ask you." Carlos' tone was full of sadness and regret.

"You didn't need to ask. I told you I loved you and I said I didn't care if you didn't have money." She was becoming upset and couldn't help her tears now welling up and stinging her eyes. "I didn't care if you don't have a big fine house for us to live in or that we would have to live with your parents. I didn't care about any of that."

He wiped away her tears with his fingers. "I know. I'm sorry. I want to make it up to you. I know now without any doubt in my heart that we can be together."

"No!" She looked at him horrified. "We can't, it's too late!" She handed the fishing rod back to him and stood up.

He stared back at her confused. "No it's not too late. Of course it's not too late. My parents know about you, they will love you.

And I'm sure your mother will like me too."

"It can't happen, not now, not ever." In a flood of tears, she ran away from him. He sat bewildered for a moment, then stood up and raced after her, but she had disappeared into the crowds and it was too late, it was impossible to find her. All he could hope for was that he would see her again soon. Now he knew that she had not gone to England, he would search for her until he found her and make her see sense that it was not too late and that they had their whole lives ahead of them.

The truth may set you free, but that's not always so. You can't undo what has already been done.

Jen put the book down and checked her watch. She had three quarters of an hour until her date with Carlos, she had better get a move on. The book was becoming an addiction. She couldn't stop reading it. It was written with so much feeling, so much conviction, although extremely sad in places and she hoped the person found happiness in the end. Surely everyone deserved a happy ending?

198

Happiness is a myth.

What? No of course it isn't. Jen, marched off towards the bathroom to take a shower, annoyed at more random sayings entering her head.

Carlos, clean shaven, slapped on some aftershave and stood back to check himself in the mirror. He was still debating if he should wear the pale blue shirt or the white one. He ran a comb through his hair, feeling nervous, wondering if he was doing the right thing. It had been three years since his wife passed, so why did it still feel like a betrayal? He could call the date off, he was very much aware of that, but Jen was also a potential client, although it wasn't about money, it just wouldn't have been nice to let her down. She had been through a difficult time recently, losing her friend, splitting up from her husband. He put the comb down again on the bathroom shelf. No, he would not cancel. It was just dinner and a couple of drinks that's all, no big deal, nothing to be nervous about.

Panting heavily, he threw open the church doors. Fortunately, there was no service on at that time of the day and apart from an old lady sitting on the front pew, who threw an unappreciative glare his way after disturbing her prayer, Carlos found himself to be alone. The English church was the first place he could think of to try and find Esperanza. He sighed heavily and feeling dejected he turned towards the door.

"Young man!" Albert Jones called out to him, making his way swiftly down the aisle.

Seeing the vicar coming towards him, he suddenly felt anxious. His English was almost non-existent, something he had not considered in his haste to search for Esperanza in an English-speaking church.

Albert, noticing that the boy looked local, spoke to him in Spanish, and he asked if he could help, puzzled why a native young man should be entering an Anglican church and not a Catholic one.

"You must mean Esperanza Rodriguez," Albert replied, realising the boy's distress in finding Dorothy's daughter. Albert frowned again. "I don't understand. Why must you find her so urgently?"

"I have to tell her something very important," Carlos disclosed, his eyes staring pleadingly at Albert's.

"Very well, if you give me your message, I will see that she receives it today."

Carlos stepped back with a look of humiliation. "What I have to say is private, it is not a message that anyone can deliver, I must speak to her myself. If you could please tell me where she lives and then I will be on my way." He stood with his arms folded across his chest defiantly. Albert surveyed him closely wondering if he could be trusted.

"Esperanza? Alfredo is here to take you to see a house," Dorothy called up the stairs. "And he is going to take you and your sisters out for dinner later too, seeing as you forgot to buy some meat or fish!" She rolled her eyes, standing with her hands on her hips waiting for Esperanza's reply.

"Alright. I'll be down soon," she shouted back, checking her eyes in the mirror. Fortunately, with a little face powder, the puffiness from crying, had been hidden. She maneuvered her hair pin to sit straight and then remembering her ring, she looked down at her bare finger. It must still be in her pocket! She ran over to the dress she had been wearing when she had met Carols earlier that day, it was strewn over the bedstead. She checked the right pocket and then the left, but the ring was gone. In a flood of panic she searched all around the bed and under it. Oh how could she have been so stupid to have lost it. She should never have taken it off. If she had only told Carlos the truth and walked away from him this would not have happened. A tap at the door made her jump. "I'm busy," she replied, irritated that her mother was hurrying her again.

Jessica entered the room, ignoring her sister's angry tone. "What are you doing?" she enquired, watching her sister scramble around on the bedroom floor.

"I've lost my ring," Esperanza blurted out, before bursting into tears.

"Oh Espe, don't panic. I'll help you find it. Where were you when you took it off?"

Their eyes met from across the room. Esperanza couldn't lie to her sister but telling her the truth was a risk if it ever got back to her mother. "I put it in my pocket, in this pocket," she pointed to the dress.

Jessica pulled the cover back with force and the ring flew through the air, landing under the dressing table.

"Oh my God! Thank you, Jess, thank you!" Esperanza collected the ring and shoved it on her finger. She held out her hand to inspect it. It was on her finger again, where it belonged, and she needed to get Carlos out of her head. She kissed her sister on the forehead and dashed passed her and down the stairs.

"Esperanza, you look beautiful, you always do." Alfredo inhaled the sweet scent of her perfume as he kissed her on the cheek.

Dorothy rubbed her hands with glee, thrilled at what a lovely couple they made.

"Well, I must get back to the shop. I hope this house you are going to see will be the one." She stood up from the sofa, smoothing the creases from her dress with the palms of her hands. "You look a little peaky, are you alright, darling?"

"I'm fine Mama."

Alfredo took a closer look at her and she turned her head in hope that he couldn't see that she had been crying, but it was too late.

"Espe, have you been crying?" He looked concerned and Dorothy walked over to her to get a better look, just as Jessica entered the room.

"No of course not," Esperanza lied. "I'm fine, please don't fuss."

Jessica rolled her eyes with exasperation. "She dropped her ring in the bedroom and couldn't find it, that's why she's been crying."

Alfredo took Esperanza's hand, "Oh you poor sweetheart. Well, you found it, I see."

"I found it," Jessica said, pointing to herself.

"I'm sorry," Esperanza apologised, relieved that he didn't know the real reason why she had been crying earlier.

"You shouldn't take your engagement ring off." Dorothy shook her head and then made her way towards the front door. "Jess, make sure you get changed and get your sister ready for when Esperanza and Alfredo get back, you are going out for dinner."

Jessica shrieked with delight and then ran off to find Anna in the garden.

Alfredo and Esperanza followed Dorothy to the door. Dorothy blew them both a kiss and made her way off down the street in the direction of the shop. It was then that Esperanza saw him standing there under a flame tree across the road, and her heart skipped a beat.

Carlos was busy preparing his speech in his mind. He had said the words over and over again and now that he had seen her come out of the house, he was determined to get it right. He ran across the road and stopped immediately in his tracks, noticing Alfredo next to her with his arm around her. Perhaps he was a relative, a cousin or something.

"Espe!" he called out, trying to fathom who the well-dressed gentleman was at her side.

"Hola," she replied awkwardly. "I'm afraid I don't have time to speak, we have an appointment to get to." Much to her annoyance she could feel the colour rising in her cheeks.

"You know this…person?" Alfredo eyed the scruffy young man before him, up and down with a glint of amusement in his eyes. Carlos was still holding a fishing rod and a bucket, which he had taken with him, not having anywhere to leave it in his rush to find Esperanza.

"Yes, this is Carlos Garcia, he works at the harbour," she said at last.

"Ah a fisherman of course," Alfredo tipped his hat in a mocking manner. "My fiancée and I don't want any fish thank you. Don't let us keep you." Alfredo pushed Esperanza gently to walk on, leaving Carlos shocked by his words as he stepped out of their way. Fiancée? He had come to tell her he loved her, that he wanted to marry her, and she was already engaged, why hadn't she told him?

Esperanza's heart was beating fast as she walked on with Alfredo. The pained expression on Carlos' face was heartbreaking, he should not have found out that way. It was unfair. She decided she would find him later and explain. And her worried expression didn't go unnoticed.

"Are you alright, darling? Has that fisherman bothered you before?" Alfredo took her hand into his own.

"No, of course not," she forced a small smile, and they continued their walk towards his shiny new motor car.

A short while later they stood at the Mirador in La Paz admiring the view of the coastline.

"It's a wonderful area, not far from your mother, your sisters, the shop. And above all, its peaceful and inspirational for a budding author such as yourself!" He kissed her cheek and she turned to face him with a smile. He was kind and thoughtful and she should be content with such a decent man who had saved her family from poverty. She owed it to her mother and to Alfredo to be his wife and a good wife at that. Looking over his shoulder she noticed the tiny church across the way.

"Oh look, what an adorable little church. Can we go inside?"

Alfredo checked his watch, they had five minutes to spare, and the villa was nearby.

But before he could reply, Esperanza was already making her way into the church. Once inside she wondered around in a daze. It was a few minutes later when he managed to steer her out of there and she looked at him, her eyes dancing with excitement.

"Can we please get married here?"

"Here?" he smirked. "It's tiny, we wouldn't fit all our guests in here."

"I don't want lots of guests," she replied indignantly. "I only want those who are important to us. Your family and mine. Please Alfredo?"

He held her pleading stare for a moment and not being able to resist, he gave an exaggerated sigh. "Very well, if it makes you happy, but we will have to invite everyone else to the reception."

"Yes, fine, no problem at all." She had no idea why the church had had such an impact on her, but it was quaint, special and she knew it was where she wanted to get married.

They turned a corner and walked along a narrow path lined with bougainvillea. And there at the end of the path was a little green gate that led to the grounds of a typically pretty, Canarian house with matching green shutters at the windows and a big wooden door with a large shiny brass bell. Esperanza stood, frozen to the spot, mesmerised by its beauty.

"I love it," she exclaimed, beaming from ear to ear.

"We haven't even gone inside yet," he grinned, delighted that at last she showed an interest after all the disastrous viewings they had experienced so far. "It only has two bedrooms but there's enough land to extend at the back to make at least another two bedrooms for when we have a family. There's also a sizable outbuilding. It has a lot of potential." Although this house was not what he had in mind, he knew it would make Esperanza happy; with it not being too big. He wanted to give her a much larger home with staff to look after her, but he understood that coming from living in a townhouse, albeit very nice, she would have felt uncomfortable living anywhere much larger and all he wanted was for her to be happy.

"It's beautiful. It has a homely feeling."

She was so enamored with the villa that she couldn't wait to get inside. They walked up the garden path towards the front door.

"Well if you like inside, it's yours. We shall call it *Villa Esperanza!*" Alfredo said, pulling the chain on the brass bell, waiting for the agent to open the door and let them in.

"I would like to make a toast," Carlos said from across the table, romantically set for two. "To good food, good wine and good company!" Their wine glasses chimed catching a glint of candlelight.

Pedro, the owner, the two waiters on duty, and a few of Carlos' friends, sat at the bar, they had great delight in seeing Carlos on a date at long last. The odd wink of the eye and wide grins were given in the couple's direction quite a few times throughout the evening, not that they paid any attention, they had been too engrossed with their animated chatter. The conversation had flowed well and they both enjoyed each other's company, and it was clear for all to see they got on extremely well. It had been a perfect evening sitting under the stars on the terrace, next to portable heaters that cast a warm orange glow over them.

After dinner they stopped at the Mirador on the way back to Villa Esperanza.

"Wow! It's so pretty at night," Jen sighed wistfully, feeling more relaxed than she had been for as long time, and a little tipsy from the red wine and after dinner brandy. Puerto De La Cruz was lit up with hundreds of tiny lights, like fairy lights shimmering on the sea. There was no wind, and the Atlantic Ocean was uncharacteristically calm.

"I have a confession to make," Carlos said.

Jen turned to face him. "Go on."

"I've not been out with anyone since my wife passed away three years ago." He swallowed the lump forming at the back of his throat, the same lump that always appeared whenever he spoke or thought of her. It was a constant fight between heart and head. Head said it was time to move on and start living again, and heart said that he couldn't.

Jen hesitated for a moment, not quite sure how to offer him any real comfort, the pain was etched all over his face. "I also have a confession," she said, trying to make light of things. "I've not been out on a date in over twenty-five years. I don't think I even went out on a date with my husband, sorry ex-husband."

He smiled wryly. "What a pair we are."

"Indeed," she sighed.

"Let's take it slow and see where this adventure leads us," he suggested bravely.

"Absolutely. I'm in no hurry."

He placed an arm around her shoulders, and they walked back up the road, past the little white church and the lane with a heavy scent of honeysuckle, until they reached the entrance of *Villa Esperanza*.

Jen dug out her key from her handbag. "Would you like a coffee?" she asked, hoping he would say yes. She didn't feel ready to go back to her empty house just yet, it had been such a lovey evening.

"I think I should go," he replied cautiously, before leaning towards her and planting two kisses, one on each cheek in the customary way, taking her off guard.

"Right, yes of course." She felt

embarrassed now. He had said he wanted to take it slow. Had she overstepped the mark by inviting him in for a night cap? "About your quote." She quickly changed the subject, acutely aware that her face was now burning red, not just from the wine but her making a fool of herself by inviting him in and he rejecting her offer. "Your quote is very reasonable, and I would like to go ahead with your offer," she said in a business manner. They had not spoken about it over dinner, neither of them feeling it would be appropriate on a date.

"Wonderful," he appeared both pleased and relieved, especially now that the awkward moment had passed. "We will start on the studio first and then the swimming pool. I can get a team together for the end of next week, if that's OK?

"Excellent! Buenos noches Carlos." She turned the key in the door and smiled over her shoulder.

"Buenos noches, Jen."

She closed the door and rested her back against the wood, feeling like a lovestruck teenager again. He was so charming, so incredibly handsome and it made her realise that she must have fallen out of love with David years ago. She felt no remorse for moving on with her life, not just tiny a bit or for moving to Tenerife. No wonder David had moved on with someone else too. Strangely, she no longer felt angry or bitter towards him for cheating on her, she just wished he had told her himself, spoken to her about it and they could have set each other free a long time ago, instead of hanging on and both being miserable for so long. With a wistful sigh she walked through into the living-room, chucked her handbag and jacket onto the armchair, and continued into the kitchen with the intention of making a cup of coffee. That was until she reached the doorway and then stopped at the sight before her. Rose petals were scattered everywhere, from the bouquet of flowers Carlos had given her. They were all over the oak wooden dining table, on the tiled floor and all over the ceramic work top, even as far at the hob which was over two meters away. She checked the patio doors; they were still locked. There was no way a draft could have come in through the kitchen.

Examining the whole bouquet, the roses were the only ones missing their petals. It was as if someone had torn them off, one by one, and then thrown them merrily all around the kitchen. This was crazy—utter madness! Perhaps when she opened the front door it created a wind through, although it was a calm night, not even a breeze she realised. She scratched her head in thought then decided there had to be a rational explanation, it would come to her eventually.

She picked out her favourite cup from the cupboard, the one with poppies, it was the same one Grace had always given her whenever she came to stay. She placed the kettle under the tap and filled it, putting it back down on the plate to boil. She then reached for the ceramic coffee jar and pulled off the lid, giving a shriek of horror at the contents. Inside, there were more rose petals, and the coffee was not coffee but soil oozing with maggots—white, fat, scaley maggots! Without thinking, she threw the pot across the room. It smashed on the tiles and she ran gagging towards the sink.

She felt her forehead, it was clammy, and her stomach was churning. Air, that's what she needed, air. Rushing over to the door, she opened it and stepped outside, glad to be greeted by the fresh air she craved. Taking deep breaths, slowly inhaling and exhaling, she calmed herself down. OK, let's think this through. Someone must have a key; they have played a practical joke while I was out—not funny. With anger now brewing at the idea of someone having been inside the villa while she was out, she walked back into the kitchen and over to the smashed coffee jar. She bent down to pick up the pieces, only to find the smell of fresh coffee rising into her nostrils. There were no petals, no soil, or maggots, only coffee. She stood up to inspect the flowers, and the roses were now all intact, there was not a single petal on the work surfaces or the hob, it was like it never happened. She stood in the middle of the room, with her hands on her hips trying to make sense of it all. Had she imagined it? How? Why? Questions were spinning in her pounding head, still feeling queasy. Was it an allergic reaction to something she ate, perhaps? Shellfish, yes that could have done it. People can get nasty reactions from shellfish. But hallucinations, is that even possible?

Ask the right questions and receive the right answers!

What? Oh my God the random words were back again. Not feeling well at all, she decided to go to bed and sleep it off, whatever *it* was.

Chapter Seventeen

The wedding ceremony had been a low key affair in the little white church of San Amaro in La Paz, just as Esperanza had wished for. In the weeks leading up to the wedding she had not managed to find Carlos, despite having visited the harbour many times and on different days. She decided that perhaps coming to Puerto De La Cruz was too painful for him, and he most probably would have heard about their wedding, it was the talk of the town. The reception had been a grand event held at a luxury mansion with over two hundred guests, it was also announced in the local newspaper. On her wedding day she had been a bag of nerves, scared, a feeling of dread in the pit of her stomach for which she could not explain, yet she knew it was the right thing to do, to marry Alfredo. There were many good reasons to marry him; he could give her and her family the security they needed, a better future for all of them, her mother and her sisters, he was kind and obviously madly in love with her. There was no reason to doubt her decision to marry him but still at the back of her mind a tiny voice screamed "help!" with each step she took walking down the aisle, until she reached his side, and when he gave her a reassuring smile and she gazed over her shoulder at her mother crying with happiness and her two sisters looking proud, she knew she must do what was expected of her and marry Alfredo.

Their honeymoon was at the Gran Hotel Ingles in Madrid. Alfredo had booked the honeymoon suite with glorious views of the city. Although he had an ulterior motive for them to go to Madrid. He had kept it from Esperanza until they had arrived, that he had managed to combine their trip with business.

"I need to spend the whole day at the shop, check on the staff and see how our new range is selling," he informed her on their first morning after arriving. Esperanza was already dressed and looking forward to breakfast then going out for the day.

"But we've only just arrived. I thought we were going sightseeing to the Plaza Mayor and the Royal Palace." She pouted her lips with disappointment.

"And we will, which is why I will get today out of the way and then I will be all yours for the rest of our stay." He planted a kiss on her lips before walking over to the wardrobe to choose one of the many suits he had brought with him.

"Oh, that reminds me," he said, pulling out a bulk of money from his wallet inside of his trousers that was strewn over a chair. "While I'm gone today, go shopping and buy yourself some clothes. And I mean proper clothes, nice ones."

She frowned, looking down at the bright yellow floral dress she was wearing. "Don't you like my clothes?" she asked, with a look of surprise.

"No I don't, you look like a child most of the time, like your mother has dressed you. You are a married woman now, married to a respectable businessman, so you need to look the part." He flashed a small remorseful smile at her, feeling a tad guilty for speaking to her so bluntly, but she really needed to know. "Oh and your hair, go to the hairdresser and get it styled."

She ran her hands over her long dark hair that was neatly braided behind her head.

"You don't like my hair either?"

"It suited you before but not anymore. You are almost twenty years old Esperanza, you need something more fashionable, chic."

"Right, fine," she retorted, picking up the wad of notes he had thrown onto the bed, not hiding the fact that she felt hurt and even humiliated that he found her style of dress and her hair to be childish.

To Esperanza's surprise she enjoyed her day out alone browsing through the many beautiful boutiques and she managed to buy three new outfits, which the shop assistant had assured her were very fashionable and extremely flattering. She stopped for a spot of lunch and then her next stop was at the hairdresser. Three hours later she stepped outside looking like a different person— elegant, even more beautiful and feeling brand new with her short hair neatly curled, framing her pretty face. Heads turned as she walked down the street and for the first time ever, she felt confident swaying her hips and smiling inwardly, wondering what Alfredo would think, and her mother too when she returned to Tenerife. The young girl had been replaced by a sophisticated and sexy young woman. She gave a chuckle out loud thinking of her mother's reaction.

After taking a soak in the bath and putting on her new silver-grey, slinky, evening dress ready for dinner, accompanied by a string of pearls that Alfredo had given her as a wedding present, she was ready. She gave herself a puff of perfume to finish her preparation while admiring her makeup, pouting her bright red lips before the mirror, and giggling out loud with happiness at the way she looked.

"My goodness!" he walked into the hotel room and placed his brief case down on the floor. " you look..." he was lost for words.

She beamed excitedly, giving a little clap of her hands.

"Ravishing," he said at last. And with that, he pulled off his tie and tore at his clothes, which soon became a heap on the floor next to them both. With a forceful shove, he pushed her onto the bed behind them, taking her off guard. She gave a small pitiful shriek. They had only made love the once, the night before and it had been awkward with it being her first time. He had been careful and respectful for which she was thankful, but still feeling nervous, she felt unprepared for it to happen again quite so soon. But there was no holding him back. He kissed her neck, while pulling her gown up and then forcefully removing her underwear. A moment later, he thrust himself into her small body with ecstasy. Esperanza lay with her eyes staring wildly at the ceiling. If this was supposed to be pleasure, it was definitely one-sided. Eventually, after an explosion of jubilation, he groaned and flopped down at her side wearily, leaving her laying on her back looking traumatized by the whole ordeal.

He propped himself up on one elbow and kissed her cheek. "You are beautiful."

She swallowed hard and looked at him blankly. "I should get cleaned up," she replied, jumping up and briskly walking away with her dress still on, but looking disheveled while untying the knot of pearls around her neck that felt like they would strangle her. She collected her underwear from the floor and dashed into the bathroom for some privacy.

"We've got a table booked at 9pm in a swanky restaurant not far from here. You are going to love it Señora Sanchez," he called out to her with a wide grin. He looked like the cat who had got the cream. His pretty bride had turned into the sexiest woman he had ever seen.

"Great!" she replied bravely. Dinner she could handle, but sex was going to need some getting used to and she hoped there wasn't more of it on the menu tonight.

Esperanza and Alfredo arrived back in Tenerife three weeks later. Despite her still struggling to enjoy their sexual encounters, the rest of the trip had been wonderful. They had visited all the sights, enjoyed afternoons lazing in the sun and dinners in the finest restaurants. She had been treated like a princess and Alfredo was enormously proud of her, introducing Esperanza as his wife at any given opportunity he had. They felt happy and reinvigorated by the time they returned to Tenerife.

"I want you to close your eyes and follow me." He led her up the small winding path towards the front door. "Stop!" he said, holding his other arm out in front of her, preventing her from falling up the steps. "Open your eyes."

Her blurry vision took a few seconds to focus on the blue floral name plate below the brass bell. Her lips stretched into a huge smile. "You did it, you kept your word and named the house after me."

"I always keep my word. Which brings us to another surprise. Come with me." He guided her around the side of the house and then stopped in the middle of the garden.

"Close your eyes again."

"Again?" she gave a small, humoristic protesting groan.

"Yes, again," he said sternly, leading her step by step towards the outbuilding in the distance. Arriving at the door he dropped her arm and said, "still keep them shut." After unlocking the door, he gently pushed her inside. "Now open."

Even with blurry eyes she couldn't believe how wonderful it all looked. He had transferred the empty room into an author's paradise. There was an antique writing desk, strategically placed in front of the window with a view of the garden and the sea for inspiration. Esperanza immediately spotted the shiny new typewriter on the desk with a stack of paper and pens and pencils in a pot next to it.

"Oh my goodness! I don't know what to say—thank you!"

Behind them was a sumptuous deep red velvet sofa with scattered cushions. A coffee table matching the same dark wood as the writing table and a Persian red and cream carpet lay beneath it. On the far side of the room, next to a tall rubber plant, stood a bookshelf stocked with all of Esperanza's favourite books. Dorothy had a hand in this, helping make the room look lovely with Alfredo's cousin—they had worked on the project from Alfredo's written instructions whilst Esperanza and Alfredo were on honeymoon.

"Do you like it?" he knew full well that she did, but he asked anyway.

"I love it!" she beamed from ear to ear. "I can't wait to get writing again." She hadn't written anything the past three weeks and her fingers were itching to get on the new typewriter.

"All in good time. You need to meet your housemaid first."

"I have a housemaid?"

He laughed at her astonished expression. "Yes of course you do. As the lady of the house and a budding author, you need staff. You will have to tell her how you want things run in the house and if you need more help, just let me know, we can always hire more maids. Oh, and we have a gardener who will attend his duties twice a week."

"Right." Esperanza stared at him trying to absorb the idea of people working for her. Life was going to be quite different to the one she had been used to.

Chapter Eighteen

"Black sacks, boxes at the ready!" Petra announced, standing with her arms full in the centre of the kitchen. "You don't have to do this alone," she added.

A small smile of gratitude appeared on Jen's face. "Thank you. What would I do without you? I really need to be braver about going into that room."

"You will get used to it once you start putting your mark on things."

"That's what I was thinking. With the workmen starting outside next week, I thought I should start making the inside more my home now."

"And there's no time like the present, lead the way," Petra said.

Both women entered Grace's bedroom. It felt cold. Jen shivered.

"Do you want me to do the wardrobe or the

dressing table and drawers?" Petra asked, trying to ignore the eerie atmosphere.

"Wardrobe please," Jen replied, thinking if there was anything personal it would be in the drawers and better it fell into her own hands.

Almost an hour in, with hardly any spoken word, each of them lost in their own thoughts about Grace, Petra reached up to the top of the wardrobe and pulled out a cardboard box.

"Ah paintings," she said, flicking through them.

Jen glanced over. "Probably the ones hanging on the wall when Grace moved in. She told me the previous owner left it fully furnished and joked about the poor choice of art on the walls."

Petra continued searching through them— a few floral canvasses that had seen better days, a couple of religious paintings, Jesus nailed to the cross, another of Mary crying sorrowfully with her baby in her arms, and then she stopped suddenly, dropping the box to the floor. It gave an almighty crash as some of the glass frames from the religious paintings smashed.

"What? What is it?" Jen, sitting on her knees next to the drawers, heaved herself up to her feet with a look of concern.

"This." Petra pulled a painting out of the box and turned it around to show her. "I think we both know who she is."

"Oh God, yes, of course! The eccentric woman in black," Jen replied, watching the young woman's dark penetrating eyes that seemed to be staring straight at her. "That would make sense."

Petra frowned. "What would?"

"Her being here, walking into the outbuilding. She may have been looking to pick up her painting or other things. She could have just asked though."

"Asked?" Petra gave a humorless chuckle.

"Yes, asked if she could go in the outbuilding. She won't be able to when it's been renovated and locked." Realisation emerged on Jen's face, looking at Petra's confused expression. "Oh I forgot, you think she's a ghost, that's what you said before, that she's a ghost."

"Yes of course she is."

"Petra she isn't a ghost. I told you before, she spoke to me. We had a conversation." Jen stood with her hands firmly on her hips, in denial. She couldn't allow herself to believe in ghosts, that went against her own beliefs that when we die, that's it, lights out. We don't come back and roam around, that was just impossible, ludicrous even. "Firstly, ghosts don't exist, and if they did, I'm quite sure they don't speak," she said, matter of fact.

"Of course they can speak. Why do you think mediums exist? They act as a communicator to the spirit world. They speak to mediums."

"Well, she didn't need a medium to speak to me. And for the record mediums are a bunch of charlatans preying on the vulnerable, poor people who are grieving a loved one."

"That's your opinion and you are entitled to it, but I beg to differ! I found great comfort talking to a medium when my husband died, and she told me things no one would have ever known about my husband. And her..." she pointed to the portrait of Esperanza, "she is a troubled spirit roaming around here, trying to get our attention for some reason." Petra gave an uncontrollable shiver and placed the painting back in the box. "What do you want me to do with these?" she asked, feeling annoyed that Jen still hung on to the belief that Esperanza was not a ghost and a living person.

Jen shrugged. "I've no idea, most are broken now," she chose not to react any further. She knew if she did, it would not end well and so it was better to say nothing at all.

"There's a church jumble sale going on at the English church—All Saints, next weekend, I can drop off the few that are OK?"

Jen sat back down on her knees and carried on with sorting the bottom drawer. "Oh no, you don't have to, I'll take them in the car, when I'm next up that way," she said, not bothering to look up.

"Fine," Petra answered curtly. She checked her watch. "I do believe it's time for a coffee break now. Shall I put the kettle on?" There was no point holding a grudge. Sooner or later Jen would come to her senses and realise that Petra had been right all along.

Jen nodded in agreement, knowing this was Petra's way of calling a truce. Before following her into the kitchen, she took another long hard look at the painting that was still poking out of the box. There was no denying, the young woman was pretty, and whoever painted her captured not only her beauty but the deep sadness in her eyes too. Jen bit her bottom lip in thought. What was she so sad about? Then the book sprung to mind. Had someone written it about her? The book was old and the woman she had seen and spoken to was not old, so it would have been impossible for her to have written it herself, but it could have belonged to a relative and she was searching for it. Perhaps the woman in the painting was her grandmother, when she was young. That would be a more sensible explanation than her being a ghost.

So many questions that need answers or maybe so many answers that need questions, for the answer was born before the question!

The sweet scent of roses drifted in on a breeze through the open window. She dropped the painting onto the bed and dashed out of the room, trying to shake the feeling off that someone had been standing next to her.

"Espe! I have a surprise for you," Alfredo appeared in the doorway of her writing studio holding a large brown package.

"Alfredo, you spoil me." Esperanza looked up from her typewriter and then rushed towards him, wondering what he had bought her this time. He seemed to enjoy showering her with gifts, although often out of guilt she noticed.

"You are my wife, I'm allowed to spoil you. Here. Open." He handed it to her.

She ripped off the brown paper, revealing a portrait of herself. "My goodness, who painted it?" She narrowed her eyes, scrutinizing every detail.

"I had it painted from a photo, by a professional artist in Santa Cruz. Do you like it?"

She didn't reply, her face clouded over.

"Well I thought you would be a little more enthusiastic." He sighed heavily, rolling his eyes with despair.

"Do you remember when the photo was taken?" she asked gingerly, in barely an audible whisper, holding back her tears.

"Yes, on our honeymoon."

"Yes, but do you remember what happened just before you took that photo?" She knew she was pushing him and possibly too far, but she was tired of him pretending it was fine to treat her the way he did.

"Does it matter?" The colour rose in his face, clearly uncomfortable with where the conversation was heading.

"It explains the sadness in my eyes," she retorted, gaining her strength to stand up to him. "So, yes I do think it matters."

"OK, then I will tell you what I remember. I remember that we had just made love. You were emotional for some reason, crying afterwards. I don't know why but, anyway, that's beside the point. We went out to dinner, had a wonderful evening; all was forgotten. I think the painting captures you perfectly."

She stared at him in disbelief. Had he really no idea why she had been so upset? And how dare he think all was forgotten? It would never be forgotten, he had hurt her, not pausing for a moment when she cried out for him to stop. Each time he took advantage of her, it was a painful reminder that she was nothing more than his own property to do with her what he wished.

"Your phone was buzzing," Petra handed Jen's mobile phone over as she sat down at the table with two cups of coffee.

"Oh, thanks." There was a text message from Carlos asking her out for a drink this evening.

Petra watched her with interest. "I predict good news or maybe a gentleman friend."

Jen blushed. "How did you know?"

"A smile that broad could only mean one thing. Do I know him?"

Jen laughed. "His name is Carlos Garcia." Just saying his name made her feel warm and happy inside. "He runs a building company, the one I'm using to make the studio and the pool."

Petra showed no recognition of the name. "Cheap price then," she said with a grin.

"I don't know about that," Jen laughed again. Then A frown creased her forehead. "He has a connection with this house."

"Really? What kind of connection." Petra took a sip of her coffee and then sat forward with interest.

"Apparently, his grandfather was in love with a woman who tragically died, here in the garden." She pointed through the patio doors to the garden.

"Really? In all the years I have lived here, I've never heard anyone speak of such a story. Perhaps she's our ghost then." Petra grimaced, immediately she had said the word ghost.

"Do you mean *your* ghost?" Jen shook her head and then took a swig of coffee. She placed the mug carefully down on the table. "There's something else, Petra. Just a moment." She dashed off leaving Petra puzzled. A moment later she was back and placed the old brown book down on the table in front of her. "I found this in the outbuilding, in an old trunk."

Petra picked it up with care and gently opened it, very much aware of its delicate state. "Oh, I can't read that. I don't have my glasses with me, and the handwriting is dreadful," she sounded disappointed.

"Yes, I know, and the pages have faded with time but there are parts that can still be read. Most of it is awfully sad. I've no idea who wrote it. Let me..." She took it from Petra and opened a random page, squinted, turned the page again and then began to read.

Tears from a burdened heart. We can't stop them no more than the clouds can stop the rain from falling. The darker the clouds the more rain that falls. The darker our thoughts the more tears that fall. But after rain comes sunshine, it always does, if not straight away but at some point. Crying is merely a release of our emotions, emotions of sadness or happiness. In her life it was nearly always sadness...

"Very profound and sad," Petra said, sitting back in her seat. "But who is this person speaking about?"

"I'm beginning to think it might be about the woman in the painting. The whole book is written in third person, so obviously written based on someone the author knew well."

"Or perhaps the author was looking at an outside point of view of herself," Petra said pensively.

"A little strange don't you think? Unless it was done on purpose so that if someone found the book, they wouldn't suspect the person who wrote it to be themselves."

"Because it is in third person?"
A complicated theory but possible." Petra said, bemused by it all.

When he kissed her, it was like no other kiss, his touch was like no other touch, tingles, butterflies, never before had she experienced such emotions of excitement, extasy and above all, adoration...

Esperanza sat with her fingers poised on the typewriter, contemplating the next line. She looked out onto the gardens and the sea in the distance. No matter how hard she tried, she couldn't get *him* out of her mind. Even the main character, the hero in her book was based on *him*. It was Tuesday, late morning, he could possibly be down at the harbour right now. But what would be the point of her going there? To apologise for the way he found out about her engagement to Alfredo? A bit late for that, she was already married.

She stood up, stretched, and walked out of her writing studio. Then remembering her own personal scribblings, handwritten in a small brown leather covered book, that had been left out on her desk, she raced back inside, collected it, and placed it back in the treasure trunk under a load of blankets she and her mother had crotched over the past few winters. It gave them something to do during the long evenings. This was where she always kept her private work, her writings from the heart. No one would be permitted to read it, not ever. Anyone who knew her well enough may have guessed it was about herself, which would be devastating, especially if Alfredo was to find it.

Lost in thought, walking past the house instead of entering it, she found herself making her way down the little path and down the steps towards the centre of Puerto De La Cruz. It was like she was on automatic pilot, being led to Carlos in a trance, a trance she could not break out of. As usual it was a hive of activity, people coming and going. Cafés and restaurants busy with passing trade. She made her way down to the harbour and past the fish stalls. The sun was bright and the reflection from the sea was almost blinding as she shielded her eyes searching for Carlos. Even if she did see him, she had no idea what she would say to him.

Looking out of place, dressed so elegantly in a chic red strappy dress she had bought in Madrid, she took off her heels and sat down on the wall, watching the fishing boats coming in and out, regretting that she hadn't brought her little brown book and pencil. This was where she always used to get her inspiration, in the fresh air, the crashing of the waves, the taste of the salt on her lips, the shrieking seagulls—it was far more invigorating than where she found herself most days now, locked away in a purpose-built writing studio.

She sat for quite some time thinking about the story she was writing, thinking about the relationship between the characters she had created. They were living out what she could only dream of now. As much as she cared for Alfredo, grateful for all that did for her, her feelings for him didn't include love, she realised that more than ever. There was no love making at all, not on her part, more of a duty to satisfy her husband's needs and she hated every moment of it. Every time he forced himself on her, it was devastating.

She sighed heavily, picked up her shoes and stood up. This was all a waste of time and she should not have come, what was she thinking? She wasn't thinking at all, obviously. But as she turned around, she jumped, startled to see Carlos standing at her side. He had seen her from a distance and made his way over to her.

"Esperanza," his greeting was cool.

"Hola Carlos," she replied, feeling the colour rising in her cheeks.

"You look different," he said, eyeing her up and down, unsure if he liked the new look. He had missed the old Esperanza so much. She didn't look like the girl he once knew and loved.

"I cut my hair," she said, feeling awkward. "Carlos, I'm sorry."

"Sorry for getting engaged to a man with money and status, who can clearly give you more than I. Not something really to be sorry about, is it? It's more than I could offer." He looked away out at sea. It hurt too much to see her standing there before him. "When is the wedding?" he asked, not wanting to know the answer, kicking himself inwardly for caring enough to ask.

She swallowed the lump forming at the back of her throat. "It was last month."

"I see." The pain was etched all over his face.

"I should go," she said nervously, slipping on her sandals.

"Why did you come here today?" He turned to face her, his eyes pouring into her soul.

She hesitated, contemplating her answer, and then decided to tell the truth. "I wanted to see you, apologise for the way you found out about my engagement. I owed you an apology if nothing more."

"You owe me nothing. I let you go." His face softened. "Had you gone to England, you would have met someone there, so what difference does it really make?"

"The difference is I'm still here. I still..." she stopped mid flow, desperately holding back her tears.

A fishwife shouted harshly out as she passed by with a basket of her husband's fresh catch, deafening both of them and they exchanged a smile. It felt like old times, trying to speak above the noise in the harbour.

"Let's walk, somewhere quieter," Carlos suggested.

She agreed, following him away from the crowds. They arrived at a clearing, a patch of land with two horses happily grazing and a couple of cockerels wondering around. There was a derelict shell of a building once used as someone's home or possibly a barn, but the land looked uncared for and appeared not to be private. The view was breathtaking of the harbour in the distance.

They sat down on an old stone wall, broken in places and covered in moss. "You were saying..." he said at last.

"There is nothing to say. I'm married now. I just wanted to apologise for not having the decency to explain my engagement." Her words seemed harsh, and she grimaced inwardly.

"Do you love him?" he turned to face her.

"It's complicated," she turned away from his questioning eyes.

He reached out and touched her arm.

"It's not complicated. It's a simple question. Do you love him?"

"I can't answer that." She wiped away a stray tear, annoyed at herself for letting him see her cry.

"You just have. Why in God's name did you marry him if you don't love him? Money? Is that what it was all about? You told me you didn't care about money."

"I don't care about money. I didn't do it for me."

"Then who for?" he rubbed his forehead trying to make sense of the situation.

"I did it for my mother and for my sisters. Alfredo gave Mama a job in his jewellery shop. He pays her good money. She has been able to pay off our debts and provide food, education, and a roof over my sisters' heads, thanks to Alfredo's generosity."

Carlos shook his head with despair. "You can't see it can you?"

"See what?"

"He did it with intention. He gave your mother a job to win you over, to have you as his wife. It was a calculated move. He bought you, Esperanza."

They both fell silent, lost in thought as the realisation of what Alfredo had done, sunk in. Eventually Esperanza stood up. "I should go."

"You aren't happy with him, are you?" he stood up in front of her and took her hands into his own.

"He's a good man," she replied indignantly.

"A good man doesn't manipulate his way

into marriage. And that doesn't answer my question."

She swallowed the lump in her throat again, and not being able to contain her tears any longer she shook her head. "No, I never wanted to marry him," she cried, falling into the comfort of Carlos' arms.

He held her tightly for a while and then she looked up at him, forlorn and distraught at the love they had once shared, that she had now thrown away. He wiped her tears with his hands and then gently cupped his palms around her face. "I will always love you, always be here for you, no matter what. Do you understand?" He moved forward and kissed her tenderly.

Standing on the doorstep Jen pulled away from his passionate kiss, surprised as he was at what had just happened.

"Do you want to come in?" she asked, gaining her breath.

He hesitated and she could see the torment in his eyes. He wanted her so much but the feeling of guilt to his late wife was there again.

"Just a drink," she smiled. "Taking it slowly as we both agreed."

"You are the most sensitive and caring woman I have met; do you know that?" He looked relieved again.

With the tension now lifted, Jen placed the key in the lock and pushed open the door. He followed her inside and they went into the kitchen. "Coffee or something stronger?"

He sat down at the kitchen table. "Coffee is perfect."

He noticed the bouquet he had bought her in the centre of the table. "They look good."

She turned to face him. "Yes, they are lovely." A troubled look appeared in her eyes, remembering what happened the other night, after their last date. She turned to finish making the coffee and he walked towards her.

"No secrets. We agreed we wouldn't keep any secrets," he reminded her.

"There's no secret."

"Then why did you look so worried when I mentioned the flowers?"

"Oh, it's nothing really."

Her eyes said otherwise, and he moved closer. "Tell me, please."

"It's silly, well it's weird to be honest."

"What is?"

"You know the last time we went out? When I came back, there were rose petals everywhere, all over the side, the floor everywhere. And..." She paused wondering if she should tell him the full story or would he think her to be insane?

"Go on," he encouraged, his brow furrowed with intrigue.

"I went to make some coffee and the coffee jar was also full of rose petals, and beneath the petals the coffee wasn't coffee but soil."

"Soil?"

She forgot at times that he didn't understand everything she said despite his excellent knowledge of English.

"Earth, you know what you have in the garden, you need it for plants."

"Ah tierra. Tierra—earth, in the coffee pot?"

"Yes, that's not all," Jen said, her eyes wide open recalling the image of the maggots clearly in her mind.

"There were maggots, like little white worms," she explained.

"Maggots yes I know." He screwed up his nose. "Oh, that's disgusting. How did they get in there?"

"That's the thing, I'm not sure it even really happened."

Carlos looked confused. "I'm sorry, you have lost me now."

"I went outside to calm down and when I came back in the petals were all gone, the roses looked normal and the coffee jar, although still broken from me throwing it across the room in shock, the earth, the maggots and the petals were gone, it was just normal coffee again."

He stepped back from her, folding his arms. She rubbed her forehead. Oh God why did she tell him, he must think her to be totally nuts.

"Jen, do you ever take any recreational

drugs?" he asked, trying to keep an open mind.

"What? No, of course not!" She stared back at him, looking insulted.

"Sorry I just needed to be sure. This sounds like a…. oh, what do you call it when you have an unreal vision of something?"

"Hallucination?" she said.

"Yes, that's the word, hallucination."

"My thoughts exactly. Maybe an allergic reaction from the shellfish."

"Ah, yes, that could be." A look of relief appeared on his face as he sat back down at the table and waited for Jen to finish making the coffee. At least she wasn't taking drugs.

"I want to show you something," Jen said, placing the coffee mugs down.

He raised his eyebrows. "And what is that?"

"I'll be right back." She dashed off to the bedroom and collected the painting of the mystery woman. She had thought about telling him about the book too but decided to wait. She wanted to read it all completely first. He might want to take it home and she wasn't ready to let it go just yet.

The sun was going down when she arrived back home. Esperanza had checked up on her sisters on her way back, so at least she would have an an alibi should any questions of her whereabouts be asked.

"Will you be dining with Señor Sanchez?" Dolores, the housekeeper that Alfredo had hired stood in the kitchen, her hands covered in flour from baking. Middle aged, a little overweight with red blushes and pepper coloured haired tied back in a bun. Her apron, under the flour, was starched so much it almost looked like cardboard. Esperanza shrugged her shoulders.

"I'm sorry, Dolores but I've no idea, he didn't tell me his plans."

"What time would you like to dine, Señora?" She asked, standing with her back straight and her shoulders pushed back in military fashion, waiting her orders.

If truth be told, Esperanza didn't want to eat at all. Her mind was too preoccupied, but it seemed rude not to, seeing as Dolores had clearly gone to so much trouble. "In an hour, if that is that alright?" she asked politely.

"In an hour it shall be," Dolores bowed her head respectfully and made her way back to the kitchen.

Esperanza dined alone that evening and then went to bed early. She could still feel Carlos' kiss on her lips, his caressing hands cupping her face. His words haunted her. *"I will always love you, always be here for you, no matter what."*

Eventually, she fell into a restless sleep, tossing and turning until the bedroom door opened and she woke with a start, gasping for air and sitting bolt upright.

"My Darling!" Alfredo hurried to her side and sat down on the edge of the bed, embracing her tightly. She wriggled free from his arms and the overpowering smell of alcohol on his breath that made her feel nauseous.

"I'm fine. Just a bad dream, please don't fuss." She glanced at the clock on the bedside table, it read 1.00am. "You are late home," she said, not really caring and wishing he had not come back at all. She would rather have slept alone.

"I had a drink with my cousin, after work."

He peeled off his clothes, one by one until he was fully naked and then slipped beneath the sheets next to her. He shivered at the coolness on his side of the bed, then rolled over to face Esperanza. "How was your day? Did you do much writing?"

"A little," she replied, stifling a yawn.

"Only a little? Writer's block?"

"Something like that."

There was a moment of silence and then he pushed her hair from her neck and kissed it gently. She squirmed and moved away.

"Espe, come on. I need you," his voice was husky and his words slurred.

"Haven't you had enough of me lately?" she retorted.

"I can never have enough of you." He glided his hand over her breasts and caressed them. "Babies don't arrive by stalk you know. They need to be made."

"Babies?" She had not even considered having a baby yet and had hoped and prayed that she wouldn't get pregnant for a very long time. "But I..."

He silenced her with a kiss. His right hand glided further down, pushing up her nightdress and separating her legs apart as he heaved himself up on top of her.

A moment later he collapsed next to her, exhausted but satisfied. He then turned his back to her and within seconds he was snoring heavily. She lay in the same position, staring up at the ceiling, tears trickling down her face.

Jen handed Carlos the portrait. He held it up to the light. He had no idea why, but her eyes seemed to move him in such a way, mesmerizing.

"Who do you think she is?" Jen quizzed, curious of Carlos' reaction.

"I think it was the woman that my grandfather loved," he replied quietly.

"What makes you think that?"

"I remember how my father described her when he told me the story. He showed me a photo in a newspaper clipping that my grandfather had kept, regarding her death. I recognise her eyes."

Jen shivered; a strange tingling sensation crawled up her spine. "She looks like the woman who came into my garden—walked into the outbuilding. The one I spoke to at the Mirador. They must be related." She still couldn't think of another explanation.

"No, I don't think the woman you saw was a relation, I think it was this woman." Carlos was still transfixed on the painting.

"But how? She'd be dead by now and the woman I saw and spoke to only a couple of weeks ago was young."

"She is dead. This is Esperanza, I'm quite sure of it." He put the painting down and looked grimly at her from across the table. "Jen, I don't want to scare you, but you were talking to a ghost."

Jen sat back in her chair, realising finally that both Petra and Carlos can't be wrong. The woman she had seen, spoken to, chased after, the woman they called Esperanza, and her villa was named after, was in fact the same woman as in the painting and she was dead. As impossible as it seemed, she had communicated with a dead person.

Chapter Nineteen

Thick mist covered the grounds of Villa Esperanza, its eerie, curling, fingers seemed to hug the house and the outbuilding on the other side of the garden. On the roof an owl landed and gave a loud hoot, it was the only sound that could be heard, other than the waves of the sea crashing below the clifftop where the villa stood detached and alone.

Jen threw out a hand, restless in her sleep. The dark figure that had been watching her from a distance moved closer. Unconscious to all that was around her, Jen sat up in bed and swung her feet to the floor. The figure seemed to be guiding her out of the bedroom and through the house. Jen, walked barefoot, not noticing the cold tiles beneath her. Her eyes, although open where not focused, her expression vacant. When she arrived at the patio doors, she instinctively pulled them back, again without recognition of what she was doing.

The figure guided her into the mist. The lawn squelched beneath Jen's feet. The owl continued to hoot and there was a rustle in the nearby bush, not that Jen noticed. The silhouette stopped, and Jen came to an abrupt halt as if knowing she could not walk any further. The dark figure, dipped in and out of the mist, around Jen, dancing and scattering rose petals like she was performing some kind of bizarre ritual. Jen could now see the shadow of the young woman, but she couldn't see her clearly enough to make out who she was or be able to touch her, she was far too fast as she danced in an out of the mist. Instead, she stood frozen to the spot, like she was in a trance, as if a spell had been cast over her and all she could do was stand and wait.

Suddenly a man's voice sounded from somewhere deep within the mist. The owl immediately stopped its calling and flapped into the night.

"Espe!" His voice became louder as he approached. *"Espe!"* Jen could sense the woman dancing around her was in danger. She could feel the fear now rising. But still the woman continued to scatter the petals although her dance had become rushed and frantic.

"Run, run for your life!" Jen shouted out, finding her voice at last and becoming increasingly scared for the woman's safety as

the man's voice grew closer and closer.

There was a banging sound, now overpowering the angry voice. The banging grew louder. Intrusive. Jen shook her head from side to side. The noise was too deafening to ignore, she wanted it to stop but couldn't find her words again. And as if someone had turned on the light, she found herself sitting up in bed, staring wildly around the bedroom; that was now a glow with the morning sunlight. Her heart beat profusely as she took deep breaths to calm herself. But the banging had not ceased, it was coming from the front door. Grabbing her dressing gown from the end of the bed and shoving her feet into her slippers, she made her way down the hallway and unlocked the door. The banging stopped at the sound of the keys. She swung it open to see a young man standing before her with several boxes.

"Jennifer Brown?" he asked.

"Yes," she replied, realising the boxes contained her belongings from England. A few moments later she found herself standing amongst the boxes in the living room. There were six in total, more than she thought there would be but even so it seemed ironic that her whole life should fit into six boxes.

Her head was throbbing, she presumed from her deep sleep and bad dream. With a heavy sigh, she plodded into the kitchen. Some coffee, breakfast and a couple of painkillers should do the trick. She would call Kate later that morning to let her know the boxes had arrived and to thank her for packing and sending them.

With a steaming hot cup of coffee in one hand and eggs on toast in the other, she sat down at the kitchen table. It was only after she took her first sip of blissful coffee that seemed to hit the right spot like a much-needed comforting hug, she glanced out at the garden, and placed the mug back down on the table with a shaky hand. No. It couldn't be. It was impossible.

In the centre of the lawn was a circle of neatly scattered rose petals. She got up and walked towards the door, noticing it was slightly open. She always made sure the door was closed before going to bed, how could it be open? Had she walked in her sleep before? Still shaking, she opened it fully and walked out into the garden. The images of what she thought was a dream spun in her mind—the woman in the shadows dancing in and out of the mist, throwing rose petals, the man calling out her name, his chilling tone, the fear she felt for the woman's safety; it felt so real yet when she had woken up it had felt like a dream. But the rose petals, the open door were definite signs of it not being a dream. She felt so confused, and her head continued to pound relentlessly.

Dreams are merely visions of the subconscious, are they not?

She spun around to find the voice that had spoken. Yet again there was no one there. Was she hearing things or were they coming from her own mind? It was all too confusing. Not being able to think anymore other than the desperate need of taking a painkiller for her throbbing head, and a lay down on the bed, she made her way back indoors.

The grandfather clock stood on the opposite side of the room; its loud tick tock seemed deafening in the silence of the house. Through the connecting doors into the dinning room, Esperanza sat at one end of a long and highly polished mahogany table, eating dinner alone again. She hadn't dinned with Alfredo for weeks, he seemed to come home later and later each night. She wondered if he was having an affair. And if he were, she wouldn't have cared. His coming home late, and lack of interest in sex recently was a blessing and a relief. It meant that she didn't have to hide her discomfort of being around him or have to lie about her whereabouts whenever she met Carlos, which was normally twice a week (Tuesdays and Thursdays), when Carlos came over from the island of La Gomera. Their secret rendezvous in the countryside were the only thing that kept her going. The long summer afternoons were spent sitting on the grass together, eating picnics she had packed, and reading her latest stories and poetry to him. They were blissful days, but they knew they would not last. One day they would have to put a stop to their meetings. But for now, they needed each other, and these were precious stolen moments that would in the future become nothing more than treasured memories they would cherish forever.

Rays of early morning sunlight peaked between the small parting in the curtains. Esperanza opened her eyes and turned her head towards the empty side of the bed. She turned her head again, her eyes now staring up at the ceiling lost in thought. A small, green, speckled, gecko sat on the wooden beam above her, not that she paid any attention to it. Alfredo had never stayed away the entire night. What if he had been hurt in an accident? He did like to speed in his new automobile.

She sat up and swung her legs to the side of the bed, then slipped on her robe, her thoughts still very much about Alfredo. And if he had been in an accident and died, she would then be a widow, leaving her free, completely free to do whatever she wanted—to be with Carlos! It wouldn't matter what her mother thought anymore. This was her life, she had done what she was asked to do, marry a man for money and not for love, but next time it would be for love. She opened the window. A delicate warm breeze entered the room. She stared out onto the grounds. From the window she could see her writing studio, the writing studio that Alfredo had made for her. And then she suddenly felt guilty. She became angry at herself that she could stoop so low as to wish her husband dead.

As she turned around, wondering who to contact first and find out where Alfredo could be, she became terribly lightheaded and a wash with nausea. The sensation grew stronger, so much so that she ran out of the room and down the hallway, stopping in her tracks and then helplessly vomiting into a plant pot, the only place she could get to on time. A cold sweat broke out on her forehead and her knees felt unsteady. She called out to Dolores for help, falling to the floor.

It was half an hour later before the doctor came and by the time he had left, Esperanza lay on the bed, tears flowing endlessly down her cheeks. She felt so confused. Trapped in her unhappy marriage with Alfredo but thrilled, much to her surprise, at the prospect of becoming a mother. But what about Carlos? Their meetings would definitely have to stop now, and just the thought of that broke her heart. Alfredo would of course be delighted, this was exactly his wish, for them to have a child. Oh goodness, Alfredo! It suddenly came flooding back to her that she was on point of trying to find out why he had not come home last night, when she had been taken unwell. What if something awful had happened to him and their unborn child would be left without ever knowing his or her father? She forced herself out of bed and got dressed.

"Yes, darling, he was here an hour ago," Dorothy confirmed from behind a stack of boxes. "He dropped off all of these for me to unpack—new stock from Santa Cruz." She popped her head over the top of one of the boxes and smiled.

"I see. And did he seem fine to you?"

"Fine?" she frowned at her daughter. "Yes perfectly, fine. Darling is everything OK? You look awfully pale."

"Yes, everything is fine. I'm just a bit tired, been doing a lot of writing lately," she lied, not wishing to divulge her worries about Alfredo not coming home last night or tell her mother her news just yet. Alfredo needed to know first.

"So, Alfredo told me. He said you are close to finishing a new novel and sending it off to the publishers. I do hope you are successful after all your efforts for so long. I would have thought you to have given up on the idea by now," Dorothy scoffed.

"I really must be going," Espe replied, not rising to her mother's bait, she had far more important things on her mind.

"Esperanza, come over and have supper with us soon. Your sisters are missing you."

Esperanza nodded. "Of course, I miss them too. Give them my love." She walked out of the shop leaving Dorothy frowning at her retreating back. She knew her daughter well, and something was not right. She made a mental note to speak to Alfredo later and see if he knew what was troubling her.

So, Alfredo had been to work, but not been home. There was only one explanation, he must be having an affair, Esperanza decided, walking back up to La Paz. More than anything she wanted to see Carlos, but it was Wednesday, and he never came to Puerto De La Cruz on a Wednesday. Arriving back up at the top of the steps, she made her way to the 'Mirador,' and sat for a while contemplating what life would be like as a mother and, also what life would be like without Carlos. Not even noticing the view of the coastline below, she pulled out a pencil and paper from her handbag and sat down to write.

Life never stands still, forever moving...

Life never stands still, forever moving forward, flowing like an endless river. If we swim up tide, we flow against it, if we swim

down tide, we flow with it. But what if we want to swim in the opposite direction? What if we don't want to go the way life is telling us to go? Surely, we must have the power to change, to swim against the tide if we so wish? Alas, it appears not. It appears that we are powerless, for when it comes to the strength of the universe and the curves that life throws our way, we shrivel and die.

Jen stopped reading and placed the book down on the sofa. She looked up at the clock and noticed it was already 4 o'clock. She had done very little due to the awful headache that had plagued her for most of the day and the images too of the rose petals on the lawn which she had no suitable explanation for, other than the fact that she was being haunted, as ridiculous as it seemed to a well-educated ex-schoolteacher who always thought, up until now that ghosts did not exist. She couldn't help but wonder if the same thing had happened to poor Grace. What if she had become so scared by Esperanza's spirit, that it had caused her a heart attack? And what if the same thing should happen to herself? She could feel her heart racing and her chest becoming tighter by the second just thinking about it. Deep breaths, Jennifer, deep breaths, in through the nose, out through the mouth. She grabbed her mobile phone from the coffee table and called Carlos. On the third ring he answered.

"Jen, hola." His soft, caring tone was comforting to hear.

"Carlos. Can I see you tonight?" she tried to hide the tremble in her voice, but she didn't do a very good job of it.

"Yes of course. Are you OK?"

"Um, yes, fine. I..." She turned around. She could have sworn someone was standing right behind her as she could feel every little hair prickle on the back of her neck. The room filled with the smell of rose scented perfume and the temperature had plummeted a few degrees. But was it her imagination running away with her?

"Jen?" his voice echoed down the line.

She brought her attention back to the phone call. "I have a couple of pizzas in the freezer. If you like pizza, that is?" She said, trying to remain calm.

"I love pizza," he replied, smiling down the phone.

Again, it felt comforting to hear his voice, she could imagine his smile and she didn't want to hang up and be alone again.

"I'll bring wine," he added. "Shall we say 8 o'clock?"

"Yes, or earlier if you want?" she bit her lip, wishing she had not sounded so desperate.

"If I finish work early enough, I will be with you at around 7.30pm."

"OK, see you then." Her voice sounded small and somewhat pathetic she thought placing the phone back down on the table, knowing she could not keep him talking any longer, especially as he was at work.

She turned around to survey the room. It was too quiet and without doubt, too creepy. But it didn't feel quite as cold now, neither could she smell the rose scent.

The boxes were still there, and she decided she should get to work with unpacking some of them, that would take her mind off things and pass the time quicker until Carlos came round.

She started unpacking them one by one. A sudden thud in Grace's old bedroom, sounded very much like something had fallen over. Jen stood up and walked cautiously towards the room, noticing her heart was pounding again. She pushed the door open and walked into the centre of the room. It was extremely cold, and she shivered. The strong smell of sweet perfume was back, the same scent—roses, and she could sense her awfully close. She turned around quickly. "Esperanza? Is that you?" Her voice sounded flat and weak in the silence of the room. Her eyes darted back and forth and all around the room, but she couldn't see her, only feel her strong overwhelming presence. With fear now rising from her stomach she turned to leave the room, stopping abruptly, giving a small pitiful shriek before throwing her hand across her mouth. There in front of her lay a trail of rose petals. With every hair on the back of her neck and arms prickling, she followed the trail, her hand on her heart, willing herself to keep calm.

The petals led back into the garden and stopped at the circle of them that were still there in the centre of the lawn from the night before. *"No! Dear God, No! I don't want to be haunted. I don't want to end up like Grace!"* Crying hysterically, she ran back down the garden and around the side of the house to Petra's villa. She hammered on her front door in a flood of tears. Petra opened it a moment later.

"Jen, what on earth..."

She threw herself into Petra's arms and sobbed uncontrollably. Petra led her indoors and into the sitting room, guiding her to sit down on the sofa.

"Jen, Jen, look at me, what has happened?"

Jen stared back at Petra through her tears, her mascara running down her cheeks. "She's haunting me," she blurted out. "The woman in black—Esperanza—she killed Grace—I know she did and now she is going to kill me."

Petra sat back, her eyes standing wide open, trying to make sense of Jen's words.

"OK," she said at last. "I'm going to pour us a glass of brandy and then you can tell me exactly what happened." She got up and made her way to the kitchen, leaving Jen alone in the living-room with the cat. The overweight ginger cat sat on the chair next to the fireplace. It sat up, stretched, and glared at Jen in annoyance for disturbing the peace. It jumped down and gave a small growl passing her at speed with its hackles up, sensing something was not right about this intruder.

Petra handed Jen a glass of brandy and sat down next to her, taking a sip of her own brandy waiting for Jen to speak.

Jen had calmed down a little now and dabbed her eyes with a tissue she had dug out of her pocket. "I'm sorry, I shouldn't have descended on you like this." Her hand shook at she brought the glass to her lips.

"Quach! Nonsense! You were obviously very scared. What happened, Jen?"

Jen inhaled and then exhaled, trying to decide where to start and so she decided only to speak of the most relevant incident.

"There's been quite a few strange happenings," she began, looking directly at Petra. "The strangest, for want of a better word, was last night. I thought I had a dream but I'm not so sure that I did."

"Go on," Petra encouraged eagerly.

"I was standing in the garden, there was a lot of mist."

"Yes, there was in the early hours on the morning. I have a weak bladder; I remember getting up at 4am and looking outside. I couldn't see a thing." Petra said, then fell quiet again.

Jen's eyes grew wider. "So, it was real then, the mist." Shaking, she took a large swig of brandy. As soon as it hit the back of her throat and she had swallowed it, gaining her composure from its harshness, she continued. "She was there, the woman in black, Esperanza. She was dancing in and out of the mist, dropping rose petals."

Petra listened; her eyebrows knitted together in a deep frown.

"Then there was a man's voice somewhere in the mist. I couldn't see him, but he sounded angry, like he wanted to hurt her. He called her name, well the shortened version I presume....Espe is what he said."

Jen suddenly looked even paler as realisation hit her. "Oh my goodness, I remember something now."

"What? What do you remember?" Petra sat forward in earnest.

"Not about last night. But I had a similar dream when I was in England. The mist, a woman dressed in black and a man looking for her, calling out the name Espe. I didn't know what Espe meant back then but now I do. Oh, Petra this is so creepy. How could I have dreamt about her before I had even come to Tenerife? Why is she haunting me? I think she did the same to Grace and that caused her to have a heart attack."

Petra looked thoughtful for a moment. "I think it's not so much her targeting you, or Grace for that matter, it's more that she has a message to give. As for what caused Grace's heart attack, I don't think we will ever know that for sure, although they did put it down to her having high blood pressure. Something is bothering Esperanza and she needs you to know what it is."

"I don't want to know what it is," said Jen, looking like a frightened child.

"Whether you do or you don't, it seems she won't stop until she has told you. The rose petals maybe significant. But you said it was a dream and then you were not sure?"

"It felt like a dream but when I got up this morning the rose petals were still there on the lawn and the kitchen door was open slightly. I always close it at night. And you just said it was misty in the early hours of the morning, so I must have been in the garden."

"Do you normally sleepwalk?"

"No, never as far as I know. She led me out there into the garden. I don't remember getting there or going back to bed. Why couldn't she just speak to me like she did in the Mirador—tell me what's wrong?"

"I suspect because you are now aware that she's dead and at the time when she spoke to you before you weren't, so she may think, should she show herself to you again in the same way, it would be scary for you," Petra said pensively.

"What she is doing, haunting me, scattering rose petals, making noises in the villa, is far scarier." Jen sighed wearily.

The tick tock of the grandfather clock, yet again, seemed deafening. Esperanza pushed her plate away and stood up and walked into the sitting room, staring out of the window at the garden. Alfredo had not been home for two nights now, no phone call, no excuse, no apology. If it weren't for the fact that she had gone to see her mother and Dorothy had told her she had seen him, she would have been frantic by now. She could feel her anger brewing every time she thought about him. How dare he treat her this way? She had been waiting two days to tell him her news, that she was carrying his baby, and he didn't even bother to come home.

She heard Dolores come into the dining room and clear the table, which was still full of food. Esperanza grimaced, feeling sorry for the woman having gone to the trouble of cooking only for no one to enjoy it. With her anger now getting the better of her, she stormed out of the house, across the lawn, not even noticing the beautiful sunset this evening. The garden was a glow of soft peach and yellow. She went straight to her writing studio. The only thing she needed was to write. It was her sanctuary, the one time she would fully escape reality and lose herself in oblivion. *Novel or scribblings from the heart,* she pondered momentarily. Novel she decided for the scribblings of the heart as she like to call them, kept in the little brown book, would be full of too much anger and resentment which would only make her feel worse if she was to write how she was feeling right at that moment. So instead, she picked up with her novel at the typewriter and lost herself in a fictional storyline, where happiness and love were a prominent feature throughout, contrary to her own life.

Carlos looked at Jen in astonishment. "That's crazy, more than crazy, that's..."

Oh God now he thought she was crazy. As if reading her thoughts, he was quick to stop and correct his choice of words. "Obviously, you are not crazy, I'm just saying the petals, the woman dancing in the mist, it's all..." He scratched his head. "I can't think of the word in English."

"Far-fetched," she prompted, realising he probably wouldn't understand that expression either. His blank stare confirmed so.

"Carlos, I know this all sounds crazy, but it did happen." If only it hadn't been windy earlier today and then she could have shown him the petals, but they were gone now, all blown away. "You were the one that told me I had spoken to a ghost. You must believe me when I say she is haunting me."

He cleared his throat with a small cough.

262

"Ok. So, supposing it is Esperanza haunting this house, where she used to live, why do you think she is doing all these things, the petals and so on?" he asked, trying to think rationally, if there could be a rational explanation to this madness.

"Petra, my neighbour, thinks she is trying to bring a message over, tell me something." She could feel her eyes briming with tears and Carlos was quick to comfort her. He moved closer to her on the sofa and took her into his arms.

"I'm scared, Carlos. Look what happened to Grace, my friend, living here alone." Her voice was muffled. She looked up at him through her tears. "This might have been the cause of Grace's death, so scared of Esperanza that she died."

Carlos frowned. "When you came to visit her, did Grace ever speak about a ghost, strange happenings like you've been experiencing?"

Jen shook her head. "Never, not once."

"And how long ago did you speak to her before she died?"

"About a week."

"And she never mentioned anything then?"

"No, nothing."

"Then the chances are this didn't happen to Grace. Besides, when Esperanza was alive, she was a good person. My grandfather would not have been in love with someone who was not nice."

Jen frowned. "Then why is she doing this

to me?"

Carlos shrugged. "Maybe your exploring around in the outbuilding, your plans to renovate, it have disturbed her."

"Yes, maybe the book," she said, thinking out loud.

"What book?" he asked.

She sighed. "I was going to tell you after I finished reading it. I found a handwritten book, a lot of heartfelt writing."

"Really? Was it Esperanza's?"

"I've no idea, but I think it could be. It's written in third person, like she was talking about someone else and very generalized, about love etcetera. She never referred to herself."

"Maybe she did that in case someone found it."

"Petra said the same."

"You told Petra, but you didn't tell me." He pouted playfully, trying to make light out of a heavy situation.

A small smile broke across Jen's lips. "I was planning on telling you."

"Can I see it?" he asked. "I would love to show it to my father."

"I thought you would say that. Yes, I will show it to you now, and you can take it to your father. I think I've read enough." If truth be told, she was beginning to think the book was creating some kind of curse. All these strange happenings had begun after she had found it. She was happy to get the book out of the house. She stood up and picked it up from the mantlepiece and then handed it to Carlos. "It's delicate so handle with care."

"Like you," he said, before leaning in and stealing a tender kiss.

Kisses are messages from the heart. Kisses are sacred. Kisses soon become memories only to be cherished by the ones we love.

"Umm what's that smell? Is it Pizza?" he lifted his nose in the air like a dog sniffing out food.

She slapped his arm playfully. "Is that your way of saying you are hungry? She grinned at him. Having him around made her feel safe and much happier. "I'll put the pizzas in the oven and top up the wine."

"At last, service in this place!" He smiled watching her walk away into the kitchen and then turned his attention to the book. "Oh, by the way," he called out before opening it. "We are going to be starting on the studio tomorrow and I've got a digger available so we can start on the pool at the same time."

"Oh, that's fantastic news!" Jen's voice echoed back from the kitchen.

With curiosity mounting, he opened the book very carefully.

Esperanza turned off the oil lamp that had been burning on her writing desk and stretched her arms high above her head and yawned. She had been writing for hours, a wonderful distraction. Wearily she left the studio and made her way through the garden, thankful that a light shone from the living room and it was also full moon, making it bright enough to walk through over the lawn towards the house. The sound of roaring waves could be heard from the sea below. The bushes rustled with night creatures going about their business and the call of an owl echoed through the sky. As she approached the back door she wondered if Alfredo had come home. Would he be in bed already? Walking into the living room there was no evidence of him having been there, no empty whisky glass, his usual night cap before bed. She turned the light off and made her way down the hall to the bedroom, and with bated breath, she turned the doorknob and pushed it open. To her relief the bed was neatly made, as she had left it that morning. It meant she had time now to get into bed and pretend (if she wasn't already by the time he came home) to be asleep, and avoid any possible advances on her, although they had been in short supply lately which she was extremely glad about. Her news, should he come back tonight, could wait until the morning. There was no point speaking to him late at night when he was unlikely to be sober.

Chapter Twenty

"Jen!" Petra shouted out from the kitchen door above the noise of the workmen. Surprisingly, Jen heard her and ran towards the door to open it for her.

Petra was carrying a tray of freshly baked biscuits. "I've made plenty, I thought the workmen might like one with a cup of coffee or tea."

"That's very thoughtful and they smell delicious." Jen took the tray from her and placed them on the side. "Perfect timing, I was just thinking about putting the kettle on. Would you like a coffee?"

"Oh yes please." Petra turned and looked back out at the garden at the hive of activity. There were four men working on the studio and a digger extracting chunks out of the garden.

"I thought they were working on the studio

first and then the swimming pool later," Petra said, turning to face Jen again, who was busy adding milk to both cups.

"Carlos had a digger available and said we might as well get started on laying the foundations for the swimming pool today."

"How exciting. I'll have to come and have a dip," Petra grinned, accepting a steaming hot cup, and sat down at the kitchen table.

"Do you want one of your delicious biscuits to go with that?" Jen pointed over at the tray on the worktop.

Petra laughed, "Go on then."

"I must say they are wonderful. Not sure the workmen are going to get a look in." Jen munched on one before placing the tray in front of them both.

"Glad you like them. So, any more strange goings on?" Petra enquired, noticing Jen appeared more relaxed, although still tired.

Jen dunked her biscuit into her coffee and took a bite. When she had swallowed the mouthful she replied, "No, thankfully, but I've not slept well these past couple of nights. I think my mind plays tricks on me at night—you know—imagination working overtime."

Petra nodded knowingly. "So, no more dancing around the garden in the early hours of the morning?"

Both women giggled. It was strange to think that now they could laugh about it but at the time, Jen had been so distraught. Petra speaking half in jest and, also in broad daylight, made it seem so surreal, as if it never happened.

"No, no dancing in the mist and no throwing of rose petals either. I think *she* has had enough of haunting me and has moved on with any luck."

"With any what?" Petra raised her voice against the noise of shouting coming from the garden.

"Any luck...What an earth is going on?" Jen watched the men through the glass patio doors. The man who had been driving the digger had stopped and was now shouting across at two other men. There was a lot of waving arms, but unless you were a native, it would have been impossible to determine what they were saying at the rate they were speaking, so ridiculously fast.

Jen pulled open the door and stepped out into the garden. "Something wrong?" She raised her voice above theirs. They stopped immediately and the man who had been driving the digger ran towards her.

"We have problem," he said, taking off his hard hat and wiping the sweat from his brow.

"What kind of problem?" Jen asked cautiously, hoping they weren't going to tell her it was not possible to make the pool after all. Petra was now standing by her side.

"Bones. We find bones."

"Bones?" Jen and Petra exchanged a mystified look.

"Animal bones?" Petra enquired.

"Dog. Someone's pet?" Jen added, thinking along the same lines.

The workman shook his head. "No. Not animals – human - human bones."

"Human?" both women replied in unison.

Jen marched over to the hole and peered in, then took a step back with a gasp in horror. He was right. It was a human skeleton.

"Oh my goodness!" Petra screwed up her face with revulsion. "That's awful."

"I call Sñr Garcia and he must call police." The workman ushered them away from the scene. The other workmen had downed tools in the studio and were also crowding around the gaping hole.

"Yes, yes of course please call him now. I need to speak with him too." Jen called out, aware of the apparent tremor in her voice.

Chapter Twenty-One

Esperanza, wearing a black dress, which she felt to be appropriate given it suited her mood of becoming a widow to love, now that she would have to say goodbye to Carlos, stared out of the window with a solemn expression. It was early morning and Alfredo had not come home again. He had been away for three nights in total and still not a word from him.

The garden was hidden under a blanket of thick, grey mist, quite common for Puerto De La Cruz. It had rolled in from the sea smothering the entire coast and covered the entire garden and house. She would have to wait until it cleared before venturing down to the harbour. And then it occurred to her that of course, Carlos wouldn't be able to come to Tenerife in his father's small boat in such conditions. She sighed, resting the palms of her hands on the windowsill, peering out of the window. Perhaps it would clear by lunchtime with any luck. It often did. And as she contemplated going through the mist to her writing studio, she heard the key turn in the lock of the front door at the end of the hallway. She checked her watch, it was far too early for Dolores, she always arrived late morning to clean the house and prepare the evening meal.

Her stomach gave a lurch, it had to be Alfredo. Walking down the hallway she saw him standing close to the door.

"I've been worried sick about you," she said, trying to contain her anger.

"I'm surprised you even noticed." His words were slurred and by the disheveled look of his attire, it appeared he had not gone to work.

She walked towards him, annoyed that he was drunk. "Of course I bloody noticed."

He swayed and looked at her, astonished at her language. She never swore. Well at least he had never heard her before.

"Where having you been sleeping? Surely, you've not been wearing that suit for three days?"

"That's what I mean. You don't even remember what I was wearing when I left the other morning. You don't look at me, you don't notice me." His remark would not have been out of place coming from the lips of a woman, Esperanza mused and would have laughed at how pathetic he looked and sounded, had it not been such a serious matter. How dare he be away for three nights without an explanation and then turn up drunk.

"It wasn't this suit," he snarled, brushing past her into the living room.

"Never mind the suit, we need to speak." She followed him into the living room.

"*We* don't, but *you* do. *You* need to speak." He pointed a drunken finger at her, as he fell heavily into the armchair.

"You are not making sense. Alfredo, I don't know what's got into you, but this is no way to treat me, your wife. And I have some news, some especially important news." She stood in front of him, looking down at him, now that he was sitting, she felt more confident.

"News? Let me guess? You've decided that you don't want to live in this tiny hovel any longer. God only knows why I let you talk me into buying this place. It's no bigger than a rabbit's hutch. Mind you, you are used to living in such conditions. I saved you and your mother from poverty."

"Shut up!" she snapped, wanting more than anything to slap him around the face, but instead she restrained herself. "Stop being so nasty."

"Nasty?" he sniggered.

"I'm... we are having a baby," she announced at last, finally getting her words out.

He looked up at her, stunned, trying to absorb her words which seemed to have a quick sobering effect on him. He stood up and she backed away, feeling uncomfortable with the smell of his breath so close to her face. The stench was quite overpowering.

"Well, aren't you happy?" she asked, waiting for his reply.

"If it were mine, yes, I'd be delighted. But we both know whose bastard it is you are carrying inside of you." He stepped closer again and she instinctively backed away.

"I...I don't know what you are talking about."

"Oh, I think you do. It belongs to that fisher boy you've been hanging around with."

"What fisher boy?" She blinked nervously and moved away from him yet again. She couldn't believe that he knew about her seeing Carlos, they had always been so discreet, but he had no right to accuse her of carrying Carlos' baby. That was not true. They had never made love, as much as they had both wanted to, but they knew it was morally wrong and that their relationship had no future. To sleep together would have made saying goodbye far worse when the time came.

"You see, I've had you followed. I know your every move." He came closer and poked her shoulder with his finger.

"You had me followed?" she had never felt so humiliated.

"Yes, I even have photos of you kissing him. Why do you think I couldn't bring myself to come home these past few nights?"

She threw her hand over her mouth and for a moment she thought she was going to be sick.

"I never, I never slept with him. I promise you that. This baby is not his," she sobbed, unable to control her tears any longer.

"You are nothing more than a whore!" Taking her by surprise he slapped her hard across the side of her face. She stumbled backwards and he advanced towards her. She regained her balance and turning towards the door, she fled through the dining room crying hysterically. By the time she had reached the kitchen, she realised he was coming after her, shouting at her to come back. She ran through the side door that led out into the garden. The mist was still thick, it felt cold and damp on her skin. If she could get to her writing studio, she could use some furniture to prop up the door and stop him from coming in until he had calmed down.

"Espe! Espe!" his voice echoed through the garden; his tone full of fury.

Fear rose from the pit of her stomach, the mist was slowing her down. She threw off her shoes to make haste across the lawn. The grass squelched with each footstep, wet from the dew that lay heavily covering the entire garden. She could hear his footsteps approaching, his heavy breathing coming closer as she tried to speed up. She held out her hands in front of her for guidance, blinded against the mist and acting only on memory and instinct of where everything was in the garden.

Alfredo, unable to see her and having

slipped twice, was becoming increasingly infuriated. She had betrayed him, made a fool out of him and now she expected him to pretend the child was his? Consumed with jealousy, it did not occur to him for one moment that Esperanza could be telling the truth, that the child could actually be his. All he could see were the images of the photos in his head. Her kissing that fisher boy, laying on a blanket, eating a picnic, laughing happily. He hated the fact that she looked so in love with him. She had never looked at him, her husband, in that way, not even on their honeymoon. She was not the innocent young girl he had fallen in love with and married. Oh no, she was deceitful.

As he stumbled on in search of her, it all made sense, she hadn't enjoyed their love making because she had been thinking of the fisher boy. His blood was boiling and something inside of him spurred him into carrying on hunting her down like a wild animal. He would make her pay for what she had done. It was as if something had snapped inside of him, something he could no longer control. It wasn't just the alcohol causing his irrational behaviour, but anger too, brewing like fire deep within his soul, feelings he had hidden since the death of his father were now rearing and Esperanza was the one who was going to bear the brunt for all of his hurt and pain. She had destroyed their love, his trust and now carrying another man's child. There could be no bigger betrayal.

"Espe!" he yelled out again.

Shaking, she reached the door of the studio and tugged at it, but it was jammed. The damp from the mist had caused the wood to swell. She gave another forceful tug, but it still wouldn't budge. To her dismay he had reached her side. Feeling his hand firmly grip on her shoulder she let out a pitiful cry, whimpering, pushing him away with all her strength and, after a moment of wrestling, she managed to struggle free and ran around the back of the outbuilding. He followed her. She had disappeared into the mist but gaining speed he caught up with her. Reaching out and pulling on her dress, it tore, and gave way, causing her to fall to the ground, knocking her head on a rock behind. Horrified, he stood looking down at her, his whole body shaking from head to toe.

"Espe?" he knelt next to her. Blood trickled from both the side and back of her head. His large hands fumbled carelessly around her neck trying to locate a pulse...

***

The mist had burned away by the glorious warm sunshine and at two o'clock Carlos made it across the water from La Gomera to Puerto De La Cruz. After helping his father unload their cargo of home grown produce from their land, he quickly made his way out of the harbour and towards the little patch of countryside where they always met. He searched the area, including the ancient wreck of a stone barn that had not been used for centuries. It was empty. Esperanza was nowhere to be seen. He checked an old pocket watch that his father had given him so that he could always be on time. It was much later than normal but surely she knew the mist would have delayed him? Perhaps she was unable to wait. He sat down on a stone and thought about her, the woman he loved so much yet would never be his. How could he have let her go, let her marry someone else? It broke his heart to see the sadness in her eyes and he wanted to make it better but had no idea how. It also hurt to think he had to wait until next time he was in Puerto De La Cruz before seeing her, if she didn't show up today.

***

Alfredo sat in the living room drinking neat whisky to calm his nerves, but it wasn't working. He shook violently from head to toe, his eyes encompassed with dark circles and his face ashen. He had sent Dolores home the moment she arrived saying he and Señora Sanchez were sick. It bought him time to think about his next move. He had no idea what he would tell people. She slipped, he didn't push her, so technically he hadn't murdered her, but he had caused her to run and fall. He needed everyone to know it was an accident, but quite how, he had no idea yet. What was he to do with her body which was now wrapped under a blanket where she had fallen? Whatever he was to do, he couldn't do it until it was dark and for now, he just had to stay put, bide his time, and think of a plan.

Chapter Twenty-Two

The red and white tape flapped in the warm breeze cordoning off the huge hole in the garden. Carlos had just finished speaking to the police. The excavation team were to arrive soon. He found Jen sitting with Petra in the living room. Immediately he walked in, she ran into his arms and he hugged her tightly, letting her cry, knowing she needed to release her emotions, it had been a stressful time.

Finally, she looked at him, clearly distressed. "I can't believe there's a body in the garden."

"I don't think you should stay here," he said, worried about her.

"She can stay with me," Petra piped up from the sofa.

"OK, good idea. I won't be home enough to take care of her, with so much to sort out, otherwise she could have come home with me."

"I am here you know," Jen said, looking at them both, forcing a weak smile through her tears. "You must think I'm pathetic, crying like this. I didn't even know the person, but the thought of a body being buried like that, it's awful."

"I think we all know who it is likely to be," Petra exchanged a knowing look with Carlos.

"If it is her—Esperanza—that's obviously what she was trying to tell me—that she was buried in the garden," Jen searched their faces for reassurance.

"Maybe," Carlos replied, but we still don't know the full story of how she died, presuming it is Esperanza."

"We may never know the answer to that," Petra added.

"They will have a good idea after they examine the bones," Carlos said, looking at them both. "Go and get some rest, you both look tired, let the police deal with this now and I'll come by and see you in the morning." He kissed Jen's forehead and gave her another hug.

"Take care of her," he whispered over Jen's shoulder.

Petra nodded.

The chill of the night air sent shivers down his spine despite the amount of whisky he had consumed. His fingers were black from the soil and his clothes stained with her blood after dragging her body from behind the outbuilding into the garden. He had meticulously saved the outer layer of the soil with grass still intact and had laid it on top of the mound of earth where her body lay beneath. He had dug deeply and placed her in an old blanket inside the grave. Standing back to look at his work, the realisation of what he had done hit him as he sobbed and wiped his tears across his mud-stained face.

A plan, he needed to work out a plan. He had already told Dolores they were sick. If he told Dorothy and everyone else the same, that they both had a sick bug, he could keep everyone away for at least a week, giving time for the garden to settle.

Waves throwing spume into the air crashed against the cliffs beneath the garden. A strong potent scent of seaweed filled his nostrils. And then it came to him. The garden, yes of course, that was it! She was gardening, still feeling unwell. She was trimming the hedge—he could leave the secateurs out, make a hole in the hedge and make it look like she fell through it to her death. If it happened when he was at work, he would have an alibi, if he reported it that evening. Her body could have been washed far out to sea by then, especially with the strength of the Atlantic Ocean. Even if she had landed on the tiny strip of shore below, the sea would have carried her out. No one walked that patch; it was impossible to even get to without a rope. He could explain to others she must have come over all faint, still unwell, and that's how she fell. A perfect plan, the best way to explain her death. No one need know the truth of where her body was, they would just presume it to have been swept out to sea.

He knelt next to the grave he had made for her and ran a trembling hand over the grass covering, giving it a final pat into place.

"I loved you. I loved you with all my heart. You made me so happy until you...." He couldn't bring himself to finish his sentence. Instead, he stood up and inhaled the sea air, tears flowing freely again, not knowing how he would ever come to terms with such a tragedy, a tragedy he considered himself to be responsible for.

Chapter Twenty-Three

The evening sun shone over the water and the sky was a glow of shades of red and orange. The small boat bobbed up and down across the sea, heading away from Puerto De La Cruz. Carlos had hardly spoken a word in two weeks now, ever since the news of Esperanza's death had been the talk of the town and he had overheard the shocking story.

His father called him over to sit by his side while he navigated the boat between two rocks jutting out of the ocean. La Gomera could be seen in the distance.

"I'm worried about you, boy," he said to his son, with a furrowed brow and a weatherbeaten face. "Your mother's worried about you too. I know you loved her, and it was a terrible accident falling from the cliff like that, but it couldn't be helped and...."

"I don't believe it was an accident. *He* pushed her. Her husband pushed her."

Carlos glanced at his father through narrowed eyes and then back out at sea, trying to conceal his pain.

"Son, you can't say that in public. You can't make accusations like that, especially you of all people."

"Me of all people? Me a poor farmer, is that what you mean?" he retorted angrily, turning to face his father again with anger in his eyes.

"No, for God's sake—she was married! If I'd known you'd been courting her while I was working, I'd a put a stop to it long ago."

"Which is exactly why I didn't tell you. You would never have understood."

"What I understand is that she's gone, and her family have the right to grieve for her. And it is not your place to challenge her husband. From the talk of the town and what's in the papers, he's a wealthy jeweller and if he did kill her—and it's a big if—you would never prove it, never win against the likes of someone like him."

Carlos knew in his heart his father was right, but the pain of losing her was unbearable and he wanted to lash out and hurt Alfredo. He had taken her away from him, snatched her from under his nose, made her unhappy and now she was dead. He would rather she had gone to live in England, at least she would still have been alive. He wiped his tears away with the palms of his hands and sat staring out at sea. His father's words were true, there was no point in challenging Alfredo, he had no proof, nor the money behind him needed to bring him to justice.

Chapter Twenty-Four

The sun beamed on the sparkling bright blue water. Jen and Alison stood at the edge of the swimming pool between the four sun loungers neatly lined up. Alison had flown in a few days ago to help her mother with the finishing touches to the studio, as promised.

"That's so cool, her face being at the bottom of the pool like that." Alison sat down and dangled her toes in the water. The mosaic, an exact replica of the painting of Esperanza, stared up at them. "What will you say if one of your guests asks who she is?" She looked over at her mother, shading her eyes from the sun.

"I will say, Esperanza, a lady who once lived in this villa," Jen replied, shrugging her shoulders.

Alison squinted. "The woman that used to live here, and that's all you will say?"

"Well what else can I say?"

"I suppose. I'm surprised it didn't make you want to sell up and leave, her being murdered and buried here in the garden." Alison shivered despite the heat of the sun beaming down on her.

"Carlos said the pathologist couldn't be sure she was murdered, only that there was a blow to her head. She could have fallen onto a sharp object."

"So how did she end up buried in the garden?"

"That we will never know, seeing as they have not been able to trace any family members."

"Yes, that's odd, don't you think?" Alison glanced back at her mother again, squinting against the sunlight.

"I mean this is an island, surely she would have some relatives still living here."

"They reckon the body had been there for around ninety-four years and she was around the age of twenty—that's a long time ago, Alison, people move on, move away."

***

A blackbird perched on top of a palm tree shaded the three men below from the heat of the sunshine. It chirped happily, bringing a sense of peace. Carlos Senior, a frail old man in a wheelchair, read from the small, brown book on his lap. The cemetery was empty apart from his son Carlos and his grandson, also Carlos. Three generations of Garcias stood side by side. They knew how important this would have been for the fourth generation Carlos Garcia, and that sadly he would never have known his true love had been found at last. Carlos Senior cleared his throat and continued to read aloud from the book while the blackbird continued to sing....

Dear sweet C.G, forever my light in the darkness. Don't cry because it is over, for it will never be over. A love so sweet, so pure, so tender—like a fire that once roared and now all that remains are its embers. As a memory it will always remain. If we are lucky, a love so precious touches us once in a lifetime but lasts for an eternity.

After the priest had recited from the bible and a string of prayers were said, the coffin lowered down into the ground. Carlos junior threw in a single red rose.

"Now Esperanza is at peace," he said, stepping back, standing with his father and grandfather. He felt honoured to be able to do this for his great grandfather.

"Father and Carlito," Carlos addressed them both, placing an arm around his son's shoulder, he had always called him Carlito in front of his father, to avoid confusion. "Esperanza is in her resting place thanks to Jen. She's a special lady and I would like you both to meet her." His father smiled knowingly, and Carlito nodded his head, understanding that she must be important to his father, he had not dated anyone since his mother passed.

"It's not been easy for me or for any of us since..." His emotions were getting the better of him again, he still couldn't speak about her easily.

"Since Mum died, I know, Dad." Carlito stepped in.

"Life is too short, you deserve to be happy," Carlos Senior croaked looking up at his son from his wheelchair. "You have our blessing."

Carlos smiled thankfully at them both. It seemed that putting Esperanza to rest had a double meaning. He finally, after three long years, felt ready to move on with his life and have a future again, hopefully with Jen at his side.

***

"Alison, it's ten minutes until the guests arrive. Have you put the coffee sachets in the room like I asked?" Jen took off her apron and hung it up on the back of the door.

Alison wandered in from the living room. "It looks like the tropics in there." She jerked a thumb over her shoulder in the direction of where she had just come from.

"Yes, well, you know how much I love my plants and now I don't have your father stopping me filling the house with them. Did you hear what I said about the coffee sachets?"

Yes, stop flapping. It all looks perfect."

"I think I should check it one last time. I can't remember if I left the ceiling fan on to keep it cool for their arrival."

"I think you did, but come on let's check." The two women walked across the lawn and past the swimming pool. "The villa is looking really lovely now, Mum. It looks like a real home."

"Thanks sweetheart, but I couldn't have done it all without your help."

Jen opened the studio door and Alison followed her inside.

The interior décor was stunningly serene, a mix of cream, beige, and coffee. A four-poster bed dominated the bedroom area with cream linen drapes matching the ones that framed the two large windows, giving way to lots of light and the warmth of the morning sunshine. At the foot of the bed stood a mink, chaise longue, on one wall a large oak wooden wardrobe and on the other, a matching oak table with tea and coffee making facilities, plus a mini fridge standing next to it with complimentary drinks. On the other side of the room a comfortable looking chocolate brown sofa with cream and beige satin cushions coordinated beautifully with the rest of the room. It offered a wonderful chic, boutique experience. Jen felt enormously proud and wished Grace had been there to see it. She would have loved what she had done with it, she was sure of that.

Jen straightened, yet again, the fluffy bedside rug which was already straight and perfect. And standing back to inspect it, her eyes strayed over the bed. Pink rose petals were sprinkled all over the pillows and flowing effortlessly down to the foot of the bed.

"Alison, don't you think the petals are a bit too much? It's not a honeymoon suite."

Alison took a closer look. "I think it looks lovely. Did you get the idea out of one of the interior design magazines I brought over?"

Jen frowned. "No. I didn't do this."

Alison shrugged. "Don't look at me.

"Well, if I didn't, and you didn't, who did?"

Realisation dawned on them both.

"OK, let her have the final touch. Afterall, Esperanza did live here before you did," Alison grinned, linking arms with her mother.

Jen patted Alison's hand. "Very, well. Let's just hope it is the final touch, we don't want her scaring off our guests." She checked her watch. "Talking of guests, come on, time to go and meet them."

Walking across the lawn, they were not aware of the dark silhouette that had drifted out of the studio behind them, rising into the sky towards the sun. Esperanza was now at peace.

What's in a name? That which we call a
rose by any other name would smell as sweet.

Shakespeare

About The Author

Claire Voet is an English author, born in Gosport across the shores of Portsmouth Harbour. As a child she grew up in Portchester in Hampshire. In her teenage years she lived in Puerto de La Cruz in Tenerife, before moving to the south coast of Spain. Claire is married and has three adult children, her daughter, the youngest, still lives at home.

Claire writes historical romance, paranormal, and mystery. Following her passion for the subject of paranormal, in 2020, Claire studied parapsychology accredited by the CMA and ABC to help further enrich her stories.

www.clairevoet.com

www.blossomspringpublishing.com

Printed in Great Britain
by Amazon

62177923R00177